"What do you hope to achieve by seducing me?"

"I wasn't seducing you," Sophie protested. "I was merely demonstrating that, given the appropriate stimuli, you were susceptible to being carried away."

"The appropriate stimuli being to bat your lashes, snuggle up to me and fall so spectacularly out of your dress?" he asked.

"That was an accident!"

Dear Reader,

We know from your letters that many of you enjoy traveling to foreign locations—especially from the comfort of your favorite chair. Well, sit back, put your feet up and let Harlequin Presents take you on a yearlong tour of Europe. **Postcards from Europe** will feature a special title every month, set in one of your favorite European countries, written by one of your favorite Harlequin Presents authors. This month we're taking you to Germany's Rhine Valley where castles and ruins are wreathed as much in legend as in ivy. Elizabeth Oldfield's novel is set in the heart of the valley, a most fitting backdrop for any love story. Enjoy!

The Editors

P.S. Don't miss the fascinating facts we've compiled about Germany. You'll find them at the end of the story.

ELIZABETH OLDFIELD

Designed to Annoy

Harlequin Books

TORONTO • NEW YORK • LONDON
AMSTERDAM • PARIS • SYDNEY • HAMBURG
STOCKHOLM • ATHENS • TOKYO • MILAN
MADRID • WARSAW • BUDAPEST • AUCKLAND

ISBN 0-373-11636-5

DESIGNED TO ANNOY

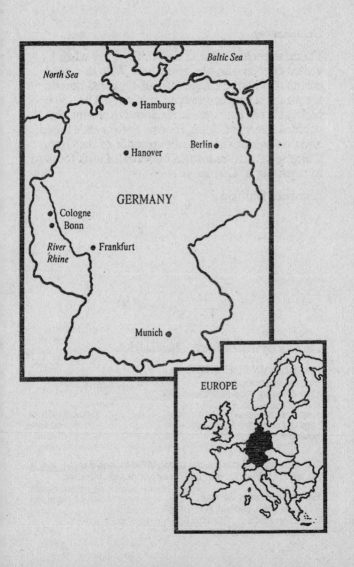

Dear Reader,

I became enchanted with the Rhine Valley when I visited friends who live near Bonn. With its ruined castles and idyllic villages of half-timbered houses, the area is scenic and steeped in history. The highlights of that first visit included exploring the cobbled streets of Bonn, touring Beethoven's home and discovering the majestic splendor of the Dom, Cologne's world-renowned cathedral. I look forward to returning to Germany!

Elizabeth Oldfield

Books by Elizabeth Oldfield

HARLEQUIN PRESENTS
1300—RENDEZVOUS IN RIO
1333—THE PRICE OF PASSION
1365—LOVE GAMBLE
1395—FLAWED HERO
1429—AN ACCIDENTAL AFFAIR
1484—STAY UNTIL DAWN

Don't miss any of our special offers. Write to us at the following address for information on our newest releases.

Harlequin Reader Service
P.O. Box 1397, Buffalo, NY 14240
Canadian address: P.O. Box 603,
Fort Erie, Ont. L2A 5X3

CHAPTER ONE

SOPHIE crouched beside the buggy. 'Von Lössingen,' she read, pointing to the stylised gold letters which were emblazoned across the smoked-glass wall of the office building. 'That's your daddy's name and in just a few minutes we shall be introducing you to your daddy, and——' apprehension clawed at her stomach '—oh, boy, is he going to get a surprise.'

His blue eyes solemn, the baby gazed up as though reflecting on the truth of her words, then he gurgled and blew a bubble.

Hoisting the overloaded backpack on to her shoulders, Sophie picked up her suitcase and holdall, and set off determinedly down the path. When she had asked the taxi driver to deliver them to the Von Lössingen headquarters on an industrial estate to the north of Cologne she had had no idea what to expect, but the complex was impressive. Over to the left, beyond acres of parked cars, stretched a red-brick behemoth which, judging from the muted internal clamour, must be the engineering factory, while to her right were workshops, warehouses and, in the distance, glimpses of docks edging the Rhine. Sophie's hand tightened around the push-bar of the buggy. What it needed now was for Rudy's father to be impressed with his son, because otherwise. . . No, she refused to think about that. Maintaining an upbeat attitude was essential.

Glass doors slid aside, and with one step the chill,

blustery February morning was left behind and she entered a calm world of air-conditioned warmth. Dropping down her case and holdall, Sophie hastily finger-combed through her long dark hair. The marble entrance hall, the chignonned receptionist, the trio of briefcased businessmen who had emerged from an elevator were all imbued with an air of sober industry, but with her tangled mane of wind-tossed curls and wearing a magenta, violet-slashed ski jacket and pants — the forecast had been snow — she suddenly felt too vivid, too casual, very out of place. And, laden with so much luggage, somewhat akin to a bag lady.

'I'd like to see Herr von Lössingen,' she said, in German, as she reached the reception desk. 'That's Herrn——'

'There's only one Herr von Lössingen here,' the girl advised, in a no-nonsense interruption. 'Do you have an appointment?'

She shook her head. 'No.'

'You need an appointment.' A desk diary was leafed through. 'Herr von Lössingen has given instructions that he's not accepting any visitors this week, so the first opportunity would be next Monday morning.'

'Next Monday?' Sophie echoed, in disbelief.

'Yes, though I'd need to confirm that with his secretary.'

After all her planning, all the expense, all the mental hoop-jumping, the reason for her journey had declared himself incommunicado for the next five days! How could he do that? she wondered, in dismay. And why? Irritation flared. From the piece-meal information she had about Johannes von

Lössingen, it seemed entirely possible that his una-
vailability could be due to his having skived off at
some earlier date which meant he now had no option
but to catch up on a backlog of overdue work. Well,
that was his problem, not hers.

'I need to see him today. I've travelled a long way
and it's important,' she explained.

The receptionist bestowed a polite programmed
smile. 'Sorry. He can't be disturbed.'

'It's *extremely* important,' Sophie insisted.

'Nine o'clock Monday morning is the first slot.'

A frown touched her brow. At a pinch she could,
she supposed, postpone the confrontation until next
week, but why should she? The current predicament
was not of her making and she resented being left to
stew by the ne'er-do-well who shouldered fifty per
cent of the blame.

'Herr von Lössingen and I are old friends,' Sophie
declared, mentally crossing her fingers.

In truth, her position was that of an associate of a
friend, but it seemed doubtful such a flimsy connection would breach the barricade which the elusive
German had constructed around him — and if a small
misrepresentation was what it took, so be it.

'Friends?' At this news, the receptionist looked
her up and down, conducting a discriminating audit
of her high-cheekboned face, her hair which foamed
like root beer, the slim, coltish figure. 'In that case,
I suppose you'd better speak to his secretary,' she
said, and closed the desk diary with a snap. 'If you
take the elevator to the fourth floor, her room is
straight ahead.'

Sophie grinned. 'Thanks.'

Inside a modern office filled with a battery of the

latest electronic technology, she found a svelte, navy-suited blonde of around forty collecting up pages as a photocopier spewed them out.

'I wish to speak with Herrn von Lössingen,' Sophie explained, when she had succeeded in man-oeuvring herself, her luggage and the baby in through the door.

'So I believe, but unfortunately it is not con-venient.' The woman gave an apologetic smile. 'Right now he's in the middle of a management briefing, and in quarter of an hour a group of visitors are due and they're scheduled to remain with him for the rest of the day.'

'Won't there be a gap after the briefing and before the visitors arrive?' she appealed.

'There could be a few minutes, but——' a protec-tive glance was cast towards a door which obviously led into her boss's domain '—I doubt he'd welcome an intrusion.'

'It'll make his day,' Sophie asserted and, shedding her suitcase and holdall, and heaving off the back-pack, she sat resolutely down on a chair.

The secretary hesitated as if about to protest, but then she sighed and completed her photocopying.

'So cute,' she said, smiling at the baby, who responded with a toothless grin.

'And very good,' Sophie praised. She unzipped his blue quilted suit and pushed back the hood. 'We flew over from London this morning,' she said, smoothing his wispy silver-blond hair into a curl on the top of his head, 'yet despite waking before dawn and being constantly hauled around he's hardly made a murmur.'

'You're English? Your German has virtually no

accent and I would never have guessed.' The secretary bent to coo over the pushchair. 'You like that?' she asked, when the baby reached out a hand and made a grab for the porcelain pendant which hung from a chain around her neck. 'Herrn von Lössingen's stepmother gave it to me,' she told Sophie, as Rudy attempted in vain to stuff the pendant into his mouth. 'Each Christmas she gives every female member of the office staff a specially chosen present—but perhaps you know?' Sophie shook her head. 'Frau von Lössingen invites us all to have dinner at her home,' explained the woman, who was clearly one of nature's chatterers. 'I so enjoy going there, though who wouldn't enjoy visiting a beautiful villa on the most elegant avenue in Bad Godesberg? First we have drinks, then a delicious meal, and afterwards——' Along the corridor a door shut and there was the sound of people going their separate ways. The briefing had ended. 'If you would tell me your name,' she said, disentangling the pendant from Rudy's grasp, 'I'll enquire whether a quick tête-à-tête would be—— Excuse me.'

The intercom on her desk had given a sudden buzz and when she answered a brisk male voice asked her to bring in the photocopies, plus a number of files, and also to collect a memo which he was completing and which he required to be typed.

'I'll go in now,' Sophie decided, as drawers were opened in a bank of filing cabinets and folders hurriedly located.

'Wait and let me check first,' the secretary said. 'He's under a lot of pressure so——'

For a second time, the intercom buzzed.

Johannes von Lössingen was under pressure—
what about her? Sophie thought mutinously, as the
voice made a request for a further file to be added
to the list. Ever since that heart-sinking, stomach-
churning moment two weeks ago when she had
realised that, after making a career of looking after
babies, she had actually been left *holding* one, she
had been agitated, anxious, plagued by fraught
imaginings which had given her restless days and
sleepless nights. No, she would not delay the confrontation a moment longer.

Rising, Sophie wheeled the buggy over, knocked
briskly, and opened the connecting door on to a
spacious, airy room. Her brown-green eyes narrowed. At a burr-walnut desk in front of the window
sat a broad-shouldered man, his fair head bent as he
wrote final sentences in a strong, determined script.
So this was the playboy of the Western world? She
raised her chin, took a deep breath, and started to
push Rudy across the cream carpet towards him.

'*Halt, halt,*' the secretary yelped, belatedly realising what was happening and cantering in after her.

The man glanced up. 'Frau Gerlach, I thought I'd
made it clear that I don't want to see anyone,' he
said impatiently.

'Yes, Herr von Lössingen, you did,' she agreed,
flustered. 'However, the young lady has come from
England and she is a——'

Sophie shone her most beguiling smile. '*Guten
Morgen,*' she said.

'Good morning,' her prey muttered in English,
then switched back to German. 'You have the
photocopies?'

His secretary retreated into her office, then rushed

past Sophie to hand them over and receive the memo. 'I'll bring in the files in a moment,' she gabbled, and rushed out, closing the door behind her.

'Thank you for sparing me a few minutes of your valuable time,' Sophie said, a touch tartly because, although she had now reached the walnut desk, Johannes von Lössingen was scanning the top photocopy and had yet to decently acknowledge her presence.

He finished reading, then pushed back his chair. 'I'm running late,' he said, speaking elegantly patterned English in a deep voice, 'so whatever it is, would you please make it snappy?'

As he strode over to a rectangular hide-leather-topped conference table which sat to one side of the room, Sophie's gaze followed him in surprise. The image she had had of the villain of the piece had been of a carefree, lackadaisical, basically light-weight character, yet this man radiated a natural authority. His manner was composed and his bearing autocratic. In an immaculate charcoal-grey suit, white shirt and dark tie, he looked focused, intelligent, professional. The gold-rimmed spectacles he wore strengthened that impression. She had also pictured him as a boyish twenty-something, but he was an adult male with an air of maturity which made it difficult to guess his age — though she would place him somewhere in his mid-to-late thirties. And the giggly, juvenile Lisette had appealed to *him*? a voice in her head protested.

But appearances can be deceptive, Sophie reminded herself, as he began to move around the table, placing a photocopy on each of the six blotter pads which, together with writing materials, a drinking glass and small bottle of designer water, were set at neat intervals. Even if words like 'solid' and 'reliable' did spring to mind his track record made it clear there was a good deal less to Johannes von Lössingen than met the eye and that he was no Mr Principles. In this case, the product did *not* live up to the packaging, she thought pithily.

'Proceed,' he ordered, when she remained silent.

Sophie moistened her lips. Although she had repeatedly rehearsed what she would say, she had not envisaged having to say it to someone so coolly self-contained, nor so forceful, and now his appearance unsettled her and made it difficult to broach the subject. Her intention had been to bowl straight in with a no-nonsense, hard-hitting indictment, yet this seemed almost like an impertinence. Also she doubted whether he would meekly accept criticism from a stranger — no matter how justified that criticism might be. She cast him a look from beneath her lashes. Unnecessarily antagonising him could prove counter-productive. What she must do, she decided in a hasty readjustment of strategy, was narrate the facts in as unaccusing and impersonal a way as possible, and leave him to take the initiative, first by acknowledging his sins and then by accepting his obligations.

'Around eighteen months ago the Von Lössingen company had a stand at an international trade fair in Cologne,' Sophie began, propelling the buggy after him because he had retreated to the far side of the table, 'and——'

'The "how to sell" bible may preach the litany of going straight to the top, but if you're plugging space

at a forthcoming English fair it's the publicity department you need, not me,' he told her.

Sophie's almond-shaped eyes opened wide.
'You're in charge here?' she asked.

'I'm the chief executive. What did you think I
was, a token family name allowed to occupy a desk
as an indulgence and window-dressing?' he enquired
sardonically.

The answer was yes. Although she knew that his
father, the founder of the company, had died several
years ago, she had assumed his presence in the office
came courtesy of nepotism. Clearly she had got
things wrong, Sophie acknowledged — some of them.
Yet if Johannes von Lössingen was a dedicated
businessman then, whatever his other faults, perhaps
he also possessed the potential to be a dedicated
parent? For the first time in a fortnight, the worry
which gripped like an iron band around her chest
eased a notch. Any kind of parent had been better
than none, but a dedicated parent was what Rudy
needed.

'I'm not selling space,' Sophie said, thinking that,
dressed as she was and toting a baby, she made a
very bizarre sales representative. 'I'm here because
of the. . .liaison which started at the trade fair.'

He thrust a puzzled glance back over his shoulder.
'Liaison?' he questioned.

She followed him as he continued to dispense the
papers. He was walking purposefully and she needed
to hurry in order to keep up.

'Relationship. The relationship with the girl who
was acting as a hostess for a London-based exhibi-
tor,' Sophie said, deciding that, although his spoken
English was flawless, his comprehension could be

less so. 'The relationship may have been in the early stages but it was close, and the girl believed it would develop into a serious commitment. That was also the impression she received when she subsequently telephoned to advise of the consequences.' She frowned at his retreating back. 'At that time, full support was promised and there was talk of setting up a home together, and the sizeable gift of cash which followed appeared to indicate that what had been said was sincere.'

Sophie stopped. The photocopies had been distributed, and now her audience was striding back to his desk where he flicked a switch on the intercom and asked his secretary to insert an additional sentence in the memo.

'Carry on,' he muttered, lowering his long body into a swivel chair.

Her lips compressed. First she had been forced to trail him around like some favour-begging supplicant scurrying after a potentate, and now, although he had seated himself, there was no suggestion that she might care to do likewise.

'Would it inconvenience you if I sat down?' she enquired, with a stiff-necked smile.

'You have my permission to stretch out full length on the floor if you wish,' he responded, frowning at a sheet of figures and opening a drawer to take out a slim black calculator, 'but please hurry up.'

Sophie parked the buggy, perched on a chair and continued. 'After swearing to stand by her, all contact ended—which was a pretty brutal way to behave,' she could not resist saying. 'I understand a lengthy Australian business trip had been mentioned and apparently, when you failed to get in touch on your return as arranged, at first Lisette thought it must've been extended, but when she rang your number had been discontinued and the letters she proceeded to send were all returned marked "gone away". Then she gave up and gave in. Not my style, but——' She halted, aware of straying from the point. 'The creation of a baby does take two and so should caring for it,' Sophie said pertinently, and paused to gauge the effect of her words.

She had expected the culprit to be sitting up and taking notice by now—looking ashamed and not a little harassed—but instead he was stabbing a long index finger at the calculator as he worked his way down the list of figures. The emerald flecks glittered in her brown eyes. How could he be so blasé and so detached? Didn't the misdeeds of his past bother him?

'Despite giving up,' Sophie carried on doggedly, 'for a long while Lisette continued to cling to the belief that, sooner or later, the prospective father would put in an appearance. Some hopes,' she remarked, derision sharpening her voice. 'Maybe you thought that terminating the relationship would result in a termination of the pregnancy?' She looked down at the rosy-cheeked child whose eyelids had begun to droop. 'Not so. All right, you could claim having Rudy was Lisette's choice, but it's not every woman who wants an abortion, and the money and the promises did prompt her to think that, somehow, things would work out and life could be happy ever after. However, now——'

'Damn,' he cursed, losing track of his additions.

He heaved an impatient sigh which indicated that *she* was to blame, then removed his spectacles.

When critical, dark-lashed eyes met hers, Sophie
stared. This was the first time Johannes von
Lössingen had been still, the first time he had taken
time out to look directly at her — and enabled her to
look directly at him. A tiny *frisson* of unwanted and
totally unexpected sensation touched her, and, for
the space of a heartbeat, she was dazzled. His eyes,
which shone a deep indigo blue, were combined with
a broad brow, firm jaw and a sculpted mouth with a
fullness which hinted at sensuality. Add lightly
bronzed skin and thick fair hair, and the man was
not only handsome, but he also possessed a powerful
sex appeal which must guarantee round-the-clock
female admiration.

As she gazed at him, a feeling of profound unease
began to gnaw at her stomach. Did his good looks
explain his failure to be troubled? Could they mean
he had got a girl pregnant and run like a stag before?
Might he make a habit of it? In a determined
gesture, Sophie hooked a shiny wing of dark hair
behind her ear. Yes or no, she was the only person
Rudy had rooting for him and she intended to do
her utmost to fight for his rights.

'However, now,' she continued, 'Lisette has gone,
which means——'

'If this visit has a point, I'd be obliged if you
would get to it,' Johannes von Lössingen interrupted
abrasively.

And I'd be obliged if you would concentrate,
Sophie thought in irritation, as his eyes drifted to
the column of figures again.

'Would it help if I spoke in German?' she
enquired.

'No need, I understand you perfectly,' he muttered, with the distracted air of a man who had other priorities. 'Though, in any case, it's been my experience that the British are not the best of linguists so it'll be quicker if we stick to English.'

Sophie's teeth ground together. He thought her German would be fractured — how condescending, how patronising, how arrogant! On the brink of demonstrating his mistake, she stopped. Despite her fluency, it was easier if she used her own language and so she would.

'The point is Rudy. All right, he was unplanned, but that doesn't mean — ' she said, then needed to break off when a knock sounded and the secretary walked in.

After depositing the memo and half a dozen files on the desk, the woman waited as her employer read what she had typed.

'Would you do sufficient copies so that everyone at the meeting can have one? *Sofort*,' he requested.

'It's nice to meet up with friends again,' the secretary remarked garrulously, as she headed for the door.

The dark blue eyes narrowed into suspicious slits. 'Pardon me?'

'*Ihre Freudin*,' she said, with a merry nod towards Sophie, and departed.

Johannes von Lössingen swept off his spectacles and rose to his feet. He had been speaking in German, but again he switched to English. 'You told Frau Gerlach you were a friend?' he demanded, coming out from behind his desk to stand before her.

'I told the receptionist,' Sophie admitted. 'It was the only way I could be granted an audience.'

'You were granted nothing. You damn near forced your way in here. Who the hell are you?' he rasped, anger hardening his voice and adding a menace to his stance. 'What do you want?'

She stood up. At around six feet three and well built, he made a formidable opponent—but she refused to feel intimidated.

'My name is Sophie Irving and I want you to take care of Rudy.'

He looked perplexed. 'Rudy?' he questioned.

Sophie gave a silent groan. She knew that when people read they were only supposed properly to absorb every sixth word, but now it seemed doubtful he had picked up more than one word in ten of her dialogue.

'What do you think I've been doing all this time— telling a sob story about a girl who got herself mixed up with one of your employees?' she enquired tetchily. 'Or quoting a case study before requesting a donation for some good cause?'

He frowned. 'One or the other, I guess.'

'Wrong. I've been talking about the girl who had the misfortune to get mixed up with *you* and who gave birth to Rudy.' She indicated the child who had now fallen asleep. 'Your son!'

The tall German stared at her, then stared down at the baby. A long pin-drop silence followed. Sophie searched his face, looking for signs of embarrassment, dismay, maybe even a dawning interest, but his expression gave nothing away. Yet a tiny betraying nerve pulsed at his temple. Watching him, she sensed that although he was outwardly controlled inside raged a maelstrom of emotions.

'My son?' he repeated at last, his voice without inflexion.

'You were aware of the pregnancy.'

Strands of fair hair had fallen over his brow, and he brushed them back with impatient fingers. 'I haven't a clue what you're talking about. Look, why don't you do us both a favour and go home and sleep this off?'

'Go home?' Sophie protested.

'To where the buffalo roam.'

'You knew Lisette was pregnant,' she protested, indignation adding a burn to her eyes. 'She rang from England and told you. I realise being suddenly faced with an offspring must be a shock —'

'A hell of one.'

'—but there's no need to play dumb. Nor to panic. I'm not just off-loading Rudy on to you and leaving.'

He gave a derisive laugh. 'That makes me feel a whole heap better.'

'I've arranged to stay with friends in Bonn for a few days,' Sophie explained, 'so that'll give you time to get used to the baby and to the idea of taking him over.'

'No, thanks.'

'Because you've managed to avoid all responsibility so far, it doesn't let you off the hook,' she told him.

'I'm not *on* any hook,' Johannes von Lössingen retorted.

At his statement, dread began to creep insidiously inside her. She had hoped — prayed — he would admit to his duties and agree to discharge them, yet neither seemed to be forthcoming.

'You think the planter of seeds should not be lumbered?' she demanded.

The nerve pulsed again in his temple and he hesitated before he answered. 'It's my belief that fathers should be there for their children,' he said, in measured tones.

'And you'll enjoy being there for Rudy,' Sophie told him eagerly. 'He's sweet-natured, rarely cries and is very little trouble. You obviously possess the resources to look after him, so——'

'I have enjoyed our chat,' he interrupted, pushing back a snowy white cuff to inspect the steel and gold watch strapped to his broad wrist. 'However, my visitors will be here at any minute.'

'A two-bit meeting is more important than the fate of your own child?' she protested, floundering between anger at the injustice and a sick sense of despair. 'Aren't you taking your obsession with business a little too far?'

'I am *not* obsessed with business,' Johannes von Lössingen grated. 'It's only a month since I went scuba-diving in the Caribbean and after Easter I intend to go——' Abruptly he stopped, as though wondering why he should be justifying himself to a stranger. 'That baby has nothing whatsoever to do with me and I shall be having nothing whatsoever to do with him,' he declared.

Sophie flinched. His words were like knives being slowly rotated in her stomach. It had always been possible that the recalcitrant father might attempt to deny paternity, but she had never imagined his denial would be so unyielding or so acid-cool.

A thought came into her head. 'Are you married?'

she asked, thinking that a newly acquired wife would go a long way to explaining this relentless rebuttal.

'No,' he snapped. 'Now please would you leave?'

'But if you're single there's nothing to stop you taking care of Rudy,' Sophie appealed, as he caught hold of the buggy, turned it around and pushed it into her hands. 'You *must*.'

'How much do you want?' Johannes von Lössingen demanded.

'Want?'

'How much money? I take it blackmail is the thrust of all this?' he said, disdain darkening his indigo eyes to purple-black.

Sophie stared, the unexpectedness of the allegation momentarily robbing her of the ability to protest.

'I'm not—not blackmailing you,' she managed to stammer.

'You didn't decide a spot of extortion would be a jolly litle wheeze? You aren't asking for maintenance? You don't want a pay-off?'

'All I want is for you to take charge of Rudy,' Sophie replied, astonished to find herself the quarry in a smear campaign. The guile and duplicity he was implying did not feature in her emotional repertoire. Indeed, the only reason she had come to Germany was because she had wanted to *help*. She had even imagined that once he had recovered from his initial surprise Rudy's father might have been appreciative. 'What am I supposed to have done, spotted a reference to your company making good profits in the business columns somewhere and thought, Eureka, big bucks!?' she enquired acidly. 'Europe may be a single community now, but isn't flying over from England in order to execute such a dastardly deed just a little far-fetched?'

'It's not as far-fetched as your claim that the child is mine. Which he is *not*!' he said, in a voice as final as a karate chop.

Her heart aching, Sophie gazed down at the innocently slumbering child. 'You can't disown Rudy,' she pleaded. 'Everyone deserves to grow up within their own family, to know their own parents, whenever possible. How do you think he's going to feel when he's old enough to realise that neither his mother nor his father were prepared to — ?' She stopped, her throat muscles locked and her eyes blurring.

'It's handkerchief time now?' the tall German derided. 'No one can accuse you of not pulling out all the stops, but, sorry, on this occasion it won't work. So what comes next?' he enquired, as Sophie swallowed hard. 'You tap-dance naked on the table?' His eyes moved down the curves of her body, blatantly divesting her of the elasticated suit and every other stitch of clothing. 'Now that might well induce me to part with a few thousand *Mark*, but another time perhaps.'

'You can deny your connection with Rudy as much as you like,' she flung at him, 'but it has no credibility. I have — '

'I don't give a damn what you have,' he interrupted.

'No, you don't give a damn about anything or anyone. All you care about is yourself,' Sophie said bitterly. 'First of all you ignore the fact that your girlfriend is having your child and may have given birth, then, even when you come face to face with him, you still refuse to acknowledge your responsibility.' She balled her fists. She had never intended to embark on a stand-up row, but she had not reckoned on such ruthlessness. Also the tears were threatening again, and she preferred to escape into anger rather than to cry. 'You, Johannes von Lössingen, are an obnoxious, callous, selfish jerk!' she denounced. 'How you can be indifferent to the plight of——'

'Johannes?' he said. 'I'm not.'

Sophie put a hand to her head in bemusement. 'No?'

'My name is Diether von Lössingen. Johannes was my half-brother.'

Stunned, she desperately attempted to marshal her thoughts. The mistaken identity explained why the man was so different from everything she had expected, but. . .

'Was?' she asked tentatively.

'Johannes died in a motor accident over a year ago.'

Sophie looked at him in horror. 'Oh, no!'

'Puts a new complexion on things, doesn't it?' he said, folding his arms across his chest.

'But—but Rudy is still your flesh and blood,' she appealed. 'He's a member of your family.'

'The relationship you mentioned—in reality it was a one-night affair?' Diether demanded.

She shook her head. 'It lasted several weeks.'

'Then how come you confused Johannes with me? OK, he had fair hair and blue eyes, but that's where any similarity ended.' His lip curled with contempt. 'Maybe bedfellows, like cats, are all grey in the dark, but could it be that you've had so many that, even in broad daylight, you find it difficult to remember one from the other?'

Sophie glared. She itched to slap his insolent face, yet there seemed a danger that if she did he might promptly slap her back.

'If you'd lent more than half an ear earlier,' she said blisteringly, 'you would know I've never set eyes on your brother and that Lisette is the girl he met at the trade fair. The girl who stayed on with him afterwards for a while and who subsequently gave birth to Rudy. The girl who rented a room in my house. The girl who, a fortnight ago, flew off to an unspecified destination in the States. The girl who left a note to say she would not be coming back,' she told him, speaking in clipped, sharp, practically spat-out sentences.

'Full marks for a vivid imagination,' he drawled.

'Sorry?'

'Much as I hate to demolish your claim, it contains one crucial flaw. Johannes died a year last October when, if she'd told him, this Lisette character must've been around two months pregnant.'

'Yes,' she agreed.

'Yet the baby can be no more than what? — six months old? — which means it's impossible for my brother to have sired him.'

Sophie's brows rose in surprise. For a man — especially a bachelor — to be able to gauge the age of an infant so accurately was unusual. Most of them tended to regard a baby as simply a baby.

'Rudy may look like six months, but he's actually nine months old. He was underweight when he was born, then suffered severe jaundice, followed by feeding problems, and that's why he's small,' she explained.

Diether gave a humourless laugh. 'You think fast on your feet.'

'It's true!'

'It's also true that you lied to get in here!' he retaliated damningly, then glanced down in surprise as a whimper sounded from the pushchair.

Rudy was squirming, screwing up his face and thrusting out a quivering lower lip.

'You've woken him,' Sophie accused.

'Me?'

'You were shouting.'

Abruptly the baby's whimper escalated into a wail, and then wails. Loud ones. His face went scarlet and he flung out his arms and furiously drummed his heels.

'I thought you reckoned he was sweet-natured?' Diether protested.

'If he's frightened by loud noises and senses hostile vibrations——' she shone an on-off smile '—you can't blame him if he cries a little.'

'A little? The noise he's making would awaken the dead,' he declared, then, as the intercom buzzed, leant over his desk to answer it.

'Signor Angellino and his colleagues are on their way up,' his secretary announced. 'Shall I ask Herrn Frischer and Herrn Kufer to join you?'

'Please.'

'And what about coffee?'

'We'll have it immediately.' He snapped off the switch. 'Would you get that child out of here?' he demanded.

'That child happens to be your nephew,' Sophie protested, bending beside the pushchair. 'Shush,' she coaxed, but Rudy's cries continued.

Diether jabbed a commanding finger at the door.
'Go!' he ordered, then he stiffened. Footsteps could
be heard, approaching along the corridor. Reaching
out an arm, he curved strong tanned fingers around
Sophie's arm and started to propel her and the buggy
towards his secretary's office.

'Don't you manhandle me!' she protested, batting
furiously at his grip, but he took no notice.

He thrust open the door and, as the secretary
looked on in surprise, bundled her ungraciously
inside.

'Goodbye!' he growled, and the door slamed shut.

'You had a. . .falling-out?' Frau Gerlach asked.

'It can happen in the best of friendships,' Sophie
said drily, and unfastened Rudy and picked him up.
'There, there, you're all right now,' she soothed,
cradling him against her, and with a shuddering sob
his yells subsided and he contented himself with the
occasional whimper.

A minute or two later, there came the murmur of
greetings in the other room, then she heard Diether
von Lössingen ask his guests to be seated.

'I must collect the coffee,' the secretary decided,
and after bidding her a smiling, '*Auf Wiedersehen*,'
she disappeared out along the corridor.

Sophie had settled Rudy back in the pushchair
and was preparing to load herself up with her
luggage again and depart, when she suddenly
realised that one of his shoes was missing. She
looked around, but without success. When he had
been crying he had kicked his feet, so presumably it
had come off in Diether von Lössingen's office —
though because of being flung out at such breakneck
speed, she thought caustically, she had failed to

notice it. Her chin jutted. She was not going to leave without the shoe.

Marching to the connecting door, Sophie knocked and entered. 'Sorry to interrupt,' she said, and, in unison, six heads turned to gaze at her.

Diether had been in the midst of start-up remarks, but he stopped dead, rose from his seat at the head of the table and strode rapidly across. 'Don't do this to me,' he said, through clenched teeth.

'I just need to find the baby's shoe,' she explained, shining a smile in the direction of his companions— all of whom smiled back.

'Then find it and get the hell out!' he growled.

The contrast of his barely contained fury with the other men's benign interest ignited a response from Sophie's mischievous streak.

'It's white and furry,' she explained, speaking in a clear voice and now shamelessly playing to the spectators, 'and I'm sure it's in here somewhere.' Her gaze travelled leisurely around. 'There it is,' she said, at last, and dropping to her knees she reached under the desk to retrieve it. 'Success!' she exclaimed, brandishing the shoe for the men to see, and, having satisfyingly prolonged Diether's aggravation, she strolled back to the door.

He marched after her. 'Come in here again,' he warned in a furious undertone, 'and——'

'You'll bind and gag me and lock me in a cupboard?' she suggested flippantly.

'It would give me the greatest pleasure.'

'Another time perhaps,' Sophie said, and with a goodbye wave to the watching men she swung jauntily out.

CHAPTER TWO

THE industrial estate was bereft of taxis and Sophie needed to hike for well over a mile, in what she hazarded was the general direction of Cologne, before one appeared. Giving her destination as, '*Hauptbahnhof* in the centre of the city,' she climbed gratefully inside. The wind blew ice-cold, her suitcase and other paraphernalia had been growing heavier by the minute, and Rudy was still grizzling.

'It's half an hour on the train to Bonn and then just a short ride to Eva's house, so it shouldn't be too long before we're there,' she said, trying to comfort him but also trying to comfort herself for now all jauntiness had faded.

Thank goodness for Eva and her husband Giles, Sophie thought, as the cab accelerated away. Thank goodness for the friendship which meant she had somewhere to stay and people who would provide the solace she so badly needed after her encounter with Diether von Lössingen. Encounter? she brooded. It had been a head-on collision which had left her feeling battered and bruised. Yet, if the man had had the grace to listen to her properly from the beginning, it need not have been that way, for then he would have realised her story was valid. Instead of which he had branded her an impostor and thrown her out. Sophie scowled. She took strong exception to having been treated in such a way, but what did she do next? Her arms tightened around Rudy. She had to do *something*.

Making a second foray into the German business-man's work environment seemed far from politic — at least for this week while he had visitors — but what was the alternative? Right now, nothing came to mind. She heaved a sigh. Time was needed to lick her wounds and bolster her spirits, so any decisions as to her next step would be left for later. Sophie peered out through the window. Eva had said that the railway station was situated beside the Dom, Cologne's gigantic Gothic cathedral, and ahead twin spires were soaring up into the heavens. They had arrived.

After paying off the taxi, Sophie joined a stream of hurrying passengers which led on to the station concourse. Finding a ladies' rest-room, she trundled inside. Rudy continued to give spasmodic whimpers and, eager as she was for them to board the train, his needs came first. A cubicle had been designated as a travellers' nursery, and here she changed him and fed him the jar of food and the bottle which had been keeping warm in her holdall.

'Happy now?' she asked, rubbing his back, and the baby replied with a burp and a contented smile.

Returning to the concourse, Sophie was studying the departures board when, among the list of desti-nations, the name 'Bad Godesberg' caught her eye. That was where Diether von Lössingen's stepmother lived, she recalled. She chewed at her lip. If the town was not too far away, should she attempt to locate the woman? Why not? Rudy was happy again, and the arrangement with Eva had only been that she would arrive 'some time' during the afternoon.

Enquiries at the information counter revealed that Bad Godesberg was an ancient spa town which served as a residential suburb of Bonn, and was just a few more miles further down the track. Sophie bought a ticket, grabbed a sandwich and a quick cup of coffee and, not much later, was seated in a warm railway compartment with Rudy on her lap, heading south. Continuing to press his case with his uncle had seemed wrought with difficulties, but his grandmother must be more receptive. Please. Please. *Please*.

Yet again, her mind returned to the scene in Diether von Lössingen's office. Why, when she had said Rudy was his son, had that pulse beat so erratically in his temple? Sophie wondered. She sighed. If he had listened to her, it would all have been so different. Though confusing him with his half-brother had not helped, she acknowledged. Nor losing her temper. Name-calling, regardless of how fraught she had been or despite it being done in error, was not the best way to win friends and influence people. If only everything could be cancelled out and they could start afresh, she thought ruefully, but there were no second chances to make a good first impression. Yet, given time to mull over what she had told him, maybe Diether would reconsider? Perhaps, even now, he was regretting his impatient dismissal and when she approached him a second time would throw himself at her feet and beg forgiveness? Her mouth curved into a dry smile. She was fantasising. Wildly. Diether von Lössingen was not the kind of man who would *ever* beg for anything.

The train had been travelling through flat farm-

land, but in the distance Sophie glimpsed forested
peaks. They would be the Siebengebirge or Seven
Hills which ranged on either side of the Rhine
around Bonn, she realised, recalling what Eva had
told her. She studied the view. This was her first visit
to one of the prettiest and most romantic regions of
Europe, and she refused to waste any more time
fretting about the hostile German. After all, if she
could find his stepmother they need never meet
again.

Bad Godesberg station was quiet. Just a handful
of people left the train and when Sophie emerged on
to the street she found one taxi waiting. Because she
did not have much in the way of an address, she
started to explain how the woman she sought had
links with an engineering firm of the same name, but
the driver cut her short. Frau von Lössingen was
well-known in the community and he could take her
straight there.

'She's the widow of Wolf von Lössingen,' he told
her, as they drove past a park and up through steep,
tree-lined roads to the top of a hill. 'She's very
involved in charity work and is on all kinds of
committees.'

'I know she has a stepson and a son who died, but
are there any more von Lössingen children?' Sophie
enquired, deciding that the more she could find out
about Rudy's paternal family the better.

She had not envisaged needing to trek from one
person to the next in search of a sympathetic hearing, but if Frau von Lössingen also dismissed her
appeal maybe it would be necessary. Though locat-
ing further relatives could prove difficult.

'There's just one other son, Axel. He's a college

student,' the driver said, and went on to tell her that the young man was regarded as a local heart-throb and how his own teenage daughter numbered among the smitten. A few minutes later, they turned into a quiet road where impressive houses were set amid well-tended gardens. 'Here you are,' he said, drawing to a halt.

They had arrived outside a mansion built in the neo-gothic style of bygone years. The walls were pristine white, while below the eaves and curving around the windows were ornate but graceful friezes and fanned embellishments painted in china blue. Blue-grey slates covered the steep-sloped roof and at one end of the house rose a small fairy-tale turret. As the cab departed, Sophie picked up her luggage and wheeled the buggy down the gravelled drive which led alongside lawns and past a garage block. Reaching the porch, she rang the bell.

'*Guten Tag*,' said the shy, timidly smiling Filipino maid who opened the door.

'I'd like to speak to Frau von Lössingen,' Sophie explained, in German.

The maid nodded, then turned as the tip-tap of high heels sounded across the parquet floor and a plump, pretty, matronly woman appeared. Her fluffy ash-blonde hair was anchored by a velvet bow, and she wore a pink cashmere dress and several strings of pearls.

'It's all right, Marie,' she said, and the maid scurried away. 'May I help you?'

'I'm looking for Frau von Lössingen—Johannes's mother,' Sophie added, determined not to make any mistake this time.

'That's me,' the woman replied, the mention of

her son's name etching a line of distress between her brows.

Sophie took a breath. 'Shortly before his death, Johannes formed a friendship with——'

Helene von Lössingen lit the gold-shaded table lamps which were placed around the drawing-room, then crossed to close the heavy dark green curtains with their big bullion fringes.

'You and Rudy must stay here tonight,' she said, coming back to lift a log from the gleaming brass basket and add it to those which flamed and crackled in the hearth.

'But he needs a cot and my friends have a cot,' Sophie protested. 'Frau von Lössingen, we'd only be in Bonn and I can bring Rudy back first thing in the morning, so wouldn't it be better if——?'

'The cot which Johannes and Axel used is still up in the attic, so he can sleep in that,' the older woman said, with a smile. 'And call me Helene, and I'll call you Sophie—if I may?'

'Please do. There'll be other things Rudy requires,' she pointed out. 'I've brought all his clothes and as many of his other bits and pieces as I could carry, but what about a high chair and——?'

'We'll go shopping tomorrow. Won't we, *mein Schatz*?' Helene crooned, scooping up the baby from where he was sitting among cushions on the sofa and hugging him tight. 'Your *grossmutter* will buy you the biggest and best teddy bear she can find. I can't begin to tell you how overjoyed and grateful I am that you've brought Rudy to me,' she said, 'but I don't want to delay you. I think if you stay a couple of days it should be sufficient for me to get myself organised.'

In just two days' time, she must say goodbye to Rudy? Sophie felt a sharp pang of distress. Over the months she had known him she had grown to love him, and now. . . She swallowed. She must not become sentimental and misty-eyed. On the contrary, she should give thanks. Thanks to Helene von Lössingen for listening to all she had had to say and believing her. Thanks that, without any need for a suggestion or a request, the woman had straight away claimed the baby and declared that his place was here with her.

'You mentioned that when you called on my stepson he was expecting visitors,' Helene went on. 'It would've been the Italians.'

Sophie nodded. 'A Signor Angellino and two colleagues.'

Some reference to her visit had seemed inescapable, though she had not gone into detail. All she had said was that, while she had introduced herself to Diether, he had been too busy to allot her any time.

'For almost two years now he's been attempting to persuade a Milan car-maker that Von Lössingen's should manufacture their components,' the older woman told her, 'and, after fighting off some very fierce Japanese competition, it's finally reached the stage where they've agreed to sit down and talk. The situation is fragile, but if your uncle Diether can persuade them to give the contract to our factory it'll guarantee jobs for lots and lots of workers for a long, long time to come,' she said, lapsing into baby-talk as she began to waltz Rudy around the room.

Sophie frowned. This was the meeting she had belittled. After his lengthy efforts the negotiations might have started badly, first because she had made Diether last-minute and annoyed, and secondly because she had disrupted everything by waltzing in to find Rudy's shoe.

'Oh, dear!' Helene exclaimed.

Startled to hear her own thoughts being verbally echoed, Sophie looked up—and saw that pearls were bouncing everywhere. When being twirled around, Rudy had clung on to, and broken, one of the strands which his grandmother wore around her neck.

'You sit down and I'll find them,' she offered, secretly relieved that the somewhat unsteady dance had come to an end.

Sophie had collected up all the immediately accessible beads and was on her hands and knees searching for stray ones beneath an armchair when a car door slammed outside. A moment or two later, the front door opened and there was the rasp of footsteps crossing the hall. As they came nearer, she glanced back over her shoulder. Involuntarily, she tensed. Diether von Lössingen was walking through the doorway, wearily loosening the knot of his tie with long, tanned fingers, in what a part of her mind registered as a sexy male ritual. What was he doing here? she wondered, in alarm. Why, when she had decided that the man could now be dismissed as no more than a bad memory, must he choose this evening of all evenings to visit his stepmother?

'Have I had one bitch of a day,' he started to complain. 'I was nicely psyched up for the Italians when some girl barged into my office and——' He stopped dead, his eyes fastening first on the baby which was being bounced on his stepmother's knee, then swooping like a startled laser beam to Sophie. His face darkened. '*Mein Gott!*' he growled.

'You've met Miss Irving before,' Helene said, in a bright, happy, bursting-with-news tone.

Fleetingly, his gaze lingered on the pert curves of Sophie's backside in the elasticated trousers before he met her eyes.

'I most certainly have,' he agreed.

Sophie clambered to her feet. Relax, she ordered herself. Think positive. You may have got off to a bad start and he may not have reconsidered, but Frau von Lössingen has accepted Rudy's validity and very soon he will too. And if he doesn't, is it cause for concern? No. The person whose feelings count in the matter is his stepmother, not him.

'Hello again,' she said, shining a luminescent smile.

'You are being a royal pain in the butt,' he told her brusquely.

'Diether!' Helene exclaimed.

He indicated the baby. 'I suppose she's told you a long involved story about this child being Johannes's?'

'But he is,' his stepmother declared, holding Rudy high in the air. 'He looks exactly like his daddy at the same age. Same little nose, same pointy ears, same rosebud mouth. And as I looked after your daddy all by myself so, *mein Schatz*, I shall look after you.'

'Did you ever hear Johannes mention a girl called Lisette?' Diether enquired.

'Well. . .no,' she admitted, 'but——'

'Neither did I.'

Sophie cast the older woman a glance. This far their conversation had been conducted entirely in German, yet now she had followed her stepson's lead and immediately switched to English. It seemed like a bad omen.

Sophie bent to lift a collection of coloured snaps from the coffee-table. 'Please, have a look at the photographs,' she said, offering them to him.

Diether frowned. 'You never mentioned photographs before.'

'You didn't give me the chance before,' she replied, purposefully keeping her tone light.

With an impatient sigh, he opened his jacket to take a spectacle case from an inside pocket. Putting on his glasses, he accepted the prints and began to leaf through.

'That's Lisette at your brother's apartment in Cologne,' Sophie explained, standing beside him, 'and Frau von Lössingen has confirmed that it *was* his apartment.'

'You must recognise it, Diether,' his stepmother said.

'I do,' he agreed curtly.

Sophie gestured to a shot of a laughing, cork-screw-curled nymph in a long gypsy skirt and with bare feet, who was sitting cross-legged on the floor. 'You can see how happy Lisette was in Johannes's company. That's her a few months later when she was noticeably pregnant,' she continued, 'and there she is with Rudy when he's identifiable as the baby who is here.'

Diether drew his glasses down his nose and

frowned at her over the top. 'There are no pictures of the girl and Johannes together,' he observed.

'That's because when her letters were returned she tore up all the snaps she had of him in a fit of pique — and not knowing what he looked like is how I came to confuse the two of you,' Sophie added. She passed him some documents which had been with the photographs. 'This is Rudy's birth certificate which gives Lisette's name and proves he is nine months old.' She pointed to the date. 'See?' she demanded.

He gave her a level look. 'I see.'

'And here is his passport.'

Diether studied the papers, went through the photographs again, and frowned, weighing things up before he passed judgement. He had to acknowledge that Rudy was his brother's son now, Sophie thought. He *must*.

'All this proves is that the girl was once at Johannes's apartment and gave birth to a child,' he said, taking off his spectacles and returning them to his inside pocket.

'But ——' she began, in protest.

'Don't you remember I told you how, just a day or two before he died, Johannes said he was going to surprise us all by settling down?' Helene cut in. 'It's obvious now that he knew Lisette was pregnant and intended to marry her.'

A sound of impatience came from the back of Diether's throat. 'At the time you were sure he meant he intended to settle down at the office.'

His stepmother pouted. 'Yes, but when Johannes rang and told me he did seem. . .excited. Far more excited than you'd ever have expected him to be if he was talking about work. And the police said the only reason they could give for his car straying off course and clipping the bridge on the Autobahn was that he'd been daydreaming. He must've been daydreaming about getting married and about the baby. And Johannes always said that if he had a son he'd call him Rüdiger, so he must've mentioned it to Lisette. Rüdiger, my Rudy,' she started to sing, jiggling the baby up and down.

'You're bending everything to fit,' Diether said, in exasperation, 'and,' he added, 'if you keep on doing that you'll make the poor kid dizzy.'

'Yes, I'm sure he'd prefer to just sit,' Sophie put in.

It was something of a surprise to find herself in agreement with him, but Rudy had been lifted, danced and bounced around so much that he was beginning to look quite pained.

'If Johannes and Lisette were merely friends, how do you explain the money?' Helene demanded, now holding the baby still.

'Money?' With a tug at the knees of his trousers, Diether sat down. 'What money?'

'You must've missed my reference to it this morning,' Sophie said sweetly. 'When Lisette telephoned to alert Johannes to her pregnancy she also mentioned that her hostessing job had folded,' she explained, sitting opposite him, 'and he said he'd send her some money to see her through until he returned from Australia. He did have a business trip planned?' she checked.

Diether gave a brief nod. 'The accident happened when he was driving to the airport to catch a flight for Brisbane.'

'Well, a few days after her phone call Lisette received the cash,' she said, in completion.

'How much cash?' he enquired.

'I understand it was five thousand pounds.'

'Five thousand?' Diether protested.

'Yes. It was far more than she ever expected or needed, though as things turned out ——'

'Johannes would never have sent a sum like that unless he was in love with the girl and she was having his child,' Helene intruded.

'But where would he have got that amount of money?' Diether demanded. He thrust his stepmother a frowning glance. 'You didn't give it to him?'

'No, of course not,' she protested, 'but he had his salary.'

'Which slid through his fingers like water,' he remarked laconically.

'It did when he was younger, but we were both surprised by how much he had in his bank account when he died, so it was obvious he'd started to save.' Holding the baby, Helene struggled to her feet. 'I shall go and tell Marie to make up a bed for Sophie,' she said and, clearly convinced that any argument was over, she walked from the room.

'You're not simply designed to annoy, you've also studied psychology?' Diether enquired.

Sophie frowned. 'I beg your pardon?'

'I don't know how you found out where Helene lived, but coming to see her was a smart move. As a bereaved mother chances were she'd be open to anything which would help keep her son's memory alive, so the odds on her falling for your story and claiming to recognise the baby as Johannes's had to be high.'

'How many times do I have to tell you——?' she began fiercely, but got no further.

'You said you "understand" Johannes sent the girl five thousand pounds?' he demanded.

'I didn't know Lisette then. We only met after Rudy had been born,' Sophie explained, 'so all I can tell you is what she told me.'

'Did she tell you how the money was sent?'

'No.'

'You said your friend left her child with you and disappeared, but what kind of person does that? Only someone who does not care. Someone with no sense of responsibility. Someone who cannot be trusted,' Diether denounced, the serrated edge to his voice making it plain there could be little doubt that *she* fitted into the same category. 'So it follows that her attitude towards sexual matters would also have been lax.'

Sophie shook her head vigorously, the chestnut curls swaying on her shoulders. 'Lisette did care about Rudy—in her way—and she was not promiscuous.'

'However, no other girl has attempted to nail Johannes as the begetter of their child,' Diether continued, as though she had not spoken, 'and he had been versed in birth control.'

'What about mistakes?' Sophie demanded. 'What about eyes meeting across a crowded room and being so gripped by desire that nothing else matters? It could never have happened to your brother, and it could never happen to you?' she added, infuriated by his disbelieving, holier-than-thou attitude. 'How wonderful to be so damn certain!'

He frowned, and in the charged silence which followed he pushed his hands into his trouser pockets and stretched out his long legs.

'Your friend could've slept with several guys,' he said heavily, 'found herself pregnant and, because Johannes looked like being the best meal ticket, told him he was responsible.'

'And for no good reason he promptly believed her and dispatched a wad of money? You think your brother was an idiot?' Sophie demanded.

'I prefer the term "hapless victim",' Diether replied stingingly.

Her eyes sparked. She could think of any number of terms she would sorely like to apply to him, yet while enunciating them might be personally satisfying it would be a waste of time. Another lambasting was not going to convince him that Rudy's cause was genuine. But if he refused to be convinced it was his tough luck, she thought, with a mental toss of her head. With Helene von Lössingen championing the baby, she had nothing to worry about.

'I apologise if I disrupted your meeting earlier today,' Sophie said, 'but I had no idea the discussions were so important.'

For a moment he looked startled by her change of subject, then he gave a twisted smile. 'I suspect the Italians enjoyed your little cabaret. Although you have yet to produce a scrap of evidence which proves that Johannes is in any way connected with the child,' he continued, 'do you think it would be prudent to give him up to Helene's tender loving care?'

'Why not?'

'She is fifty-five.'

'Which isn't that old,' Sophie protested.

'It's old to take on a baby. She'll be in her seventies when he's in his teens,' Diether pointed out, 'and my stepmother is the kind of woman who fusses and spoils.'

'A little spoiling never did anyone any harm.'

He changed tack. 'Has she indicated the least awareness of the strains, stresses and sheer *upheaval* which a child would inevitably bring in its wake?' he enquired.

Her brow creased. Helene von Lössingen's acceptance of her grandson might have been accommodatingly enthusiastic and yet, on reflection, it had also been a touch precipitate and lacking in thought.

'No, but at present she's in a state of euphoria,' Sophie defended, 'and when she calms down she'll realise——'

'What will she realise?' he interrupted. 'That the bridge games and socialising she enjoys so much are at risk, and that the time she spends in fund-raising will need to be curtailed? I'm sure she will.'

'That's a threat—right?'

'It's an observation,' Diether replied coolly.

'So what do you suggest I do—take Rudy back to England, advise the Social Services that he's been abandoned, and ask them to place him in a children's home or with foster parents?' Sophie demanded.

He scowled, restlessly moving his hands in his pockets and drawing the material of his dark trousers tight across his thighs. 'You're trying to lay guilt on me,' he said.

'I'm telling you the alternative to Frau von

Lössingen looking after him! If Lisette had had a family I could've approached them, but her parents separated when she was young. After the divorce she lost touch with her father and her mother died when she was in her teens. If I could keep Rudy myself, believe me, I would,' Sophie went on, 'but apart from the fact that, because I'm single and unrelated, the authorities would never allow it, I need to earn a living so——'

'What do you do?' Diether enquired.

'I'm a children's nanny.' She hesitated, frowning. 'Or I was until a few months ago.'

'So you're out of work?'

'I am, though it doesn't equate with "on the make",' Sophie replied tartly, for that seemed to be the implication.

'Why did you leave your job?' The indigo eyes narrowed. 'Or were you *made* to leave?'

To her fury and dismay, she felt a wash of colour rise up her face. Why must he be so suspicious and, in this instance, so accurate?

'My career is my business. Your stepmother has no problem in believing me,' she continued quickly, 'so why is it you find it so difficult?'

'Because I'm far less gullible and a darn sight more cautious. Helene may be willing to allow a total stranger to walk in off the streets and straight into her home but, in today's world, to me that seems. . .' he paused, selecting an apt English word '. . .foolhardy.'

Sophie had to admit that he had a point. And if she needed an example all she had to do was think of how she had allowed Lisette to walk in off the streets and the consequences! Yet surely he could see that she did not come equipped with horns and a tail? Surely he must recognise that *she* was bona fide? Obviously not.

'Then it's just as well I shall be staying in Frau von Lössingen's home and not yours,' she remarked frigidly.

'You are in my home,' Diether replied.

'You live here, in this house?' Sophie asked.

He nodded. 'I moved back in a couple of years ago.'

Her stomach clenched. She did not respond well to being where she was not wanted and the prospect of residing under the glare of his disapproval — even for a short time — filled her with dismay.

'Aren't you rather old to be living with your stepmother?' Sophie enquired, somewhat corrosively.

'Maybe, but it means I'm on hand to offer her my advice and my protection. You're obviously a bright girl, so let me pay you the compliment of being blunt,' Diether continued. 'You've arrived out of the blue with a story you cannot substantiate. I don't deny that there's a possibility you may be telling the truth——'

'Thank you!'

'However, there could be several other scenarios.'

'Such as?' she demanded.

'You and this Lisette could be in league, and the two of you could've decided to capitalise on her knowing Johannes and then having a baby by you insinuating yourself here.'

'But why would I insinuate myself, as you put it?' Sophie asked. 'Why not her?'

'Perhaps because you tell a better tale, and

because——' his eyes toured her rose-petal complexion, her dark arched brows, her full mouth '— you're better-looking and much classier. A stunner, in fact. Or your friend could've disappeared, as you say, and you've recognised an opportunity to create mayhem,' Diether completed.

'What kind of mayhem?' she demanded belligerently.

If anyone else had described her as 'a stunner', she would have regarded it as a compliment, but coming from his lips it was defamation.

'I don't know, but you could be a danger.'

'Perhaps you'd like to search my luggage for guns or explosives?' Sophie enquired, with a razor-blade smile. 'Perhaps you'd like to search me?'

His gaze moved leisurely down her body. Beneath her anorak she had worn a white skinny-ribbed sweater, and now his eyes lingered on the pout of her breasts beneath the knitted material before carrying on to her waist, slim hips and the legs which went on forever.

'That's a tempting offer to make to a red-blooded male,' Diether drawled.

She flushed. 'Look, I wish I could substantiate everything, too, but without Johannes and Lisette it's impossible,' she said, then stopped as Helene came into the room.

'Marie's making up your bed and I thought I'd put Rudy in the room next to mine,' her hostess announced, 'then, if he wakes up in the night, I can see to him.'

Sophie bit down on her dismay. If the baby woke up in strange surroundings, she felt sure he would want *her*—but common sense insisted he must become familiar with his grandmother as soon as possible.

'I've turned up out of nowhere and you know nothing about me, so to allay any fears of malpractice,' she said, spearing a look at Diether, 'I'd like to supply a character reference. I'm sure my friends in Bonn will be happy to vouch for me. I need to speak to them myself to tell them about the change in arrangements, so why don't you —— ?'

'A reference is not necessary,' Helene said, looking highly embarrassed. 'Diether, I don't know what you've been saying, but this is *my* house and, on this occasion, I insist on doing things my way. I *insist*,' she repeated.

He hesitated for a moment, but then he moved his shoulders. 'Just don't get too attached to the child,' he warned, 'because there's a chance you may have to give him up.'

'You think his mother could return and claim him?' she asked, in alarm.

'Either that, or ——'

'Lisette isn't coming back,' Sophie said, fending off the 'or' which seemed to forewarn of yet another assault on her honesty.

'So you're safe here with me,' the older woman told Rudy.

'But not that safe,' Diether remarked pungently, 'because if Helene continues to wear those high heels there's always a chance she could trip and drop you.'

His stepmother placed the baby back among the cushions. 'Maybe I should wear flat shoes when I carry him,' she said.

'It'd be sensible,' Sophie agreed. 'I'll need to tell

you what Rudy likes to eat, his daily routine, and explain about the innoculations he's had,' she continued, recognising a chance to draw attention to some of the practicalities. 'And suppose I give you a refresher course in changing and bathing a baby?'

The older woman frowned, as though only now realising it was over twenty years since she had performed such tasks and that she could be out of practice. 'Yes, please.'

'And you'll need a child-proof fire-guard. Rudy isn't crawling yet, but it won't be long. And a car seat, and——'

'Could you make a shopping list of everything you think is necessary?' Helene appealed. 'And instead of two days, would you be able to stay for a week?'

Sophie hesitated. Her head might insist that she should make the break as soon as possible, but the opportunity to spend more time with Rudy and make sure he was comfortably installed went straight to her heart.

'I'd be happy to,' she said, with a smile.

'Who's going to stay for a week?' a voice enquired, and a young man in suede-trimmed purple tracksuit and trainers strolled into the room. His flaxen hair was worn in a trendy gelled style and he walked with the slight but unmistakable swagger of a youth whose greatest problem in life was fighting off the girls.

'Sophie, this is my son Axel,' Helene said, and introduced them. 'And this is Rudy, Johannes's baby,' she informed the newcomer.

For a long moment he gazed at the child in stunned incredulity, then he burst out laughing. 'The

sneaky so-and-so!' he exclaimed, speaking English
like everyone else.

'Rudy is the son of Lisette, your brother's girlfriend,' Sophie explained hastily, when amused eyes
swung in her direction and she received an appreciative once-over, 'but she's vanished, so——'

'So he's come to live with his grandma,' Helene
said, kissing the top of Rudy's head. 'Diether, we
need the cot and it's somewhere in the attic. Could
you find it?'

He looked at his watch. 'I'm wining and dining
the Italians, and before I go out I need to shower
and change. So maybe Axel'll bring it down?'

The young man nodded. 'Will do.'

'Thank you, darling,' Helene said, and took hold
of his arm. 'Let's see if we can find it now.'

'Nice work,' Diether murmured, when mother
and son had departed.

'Sorry?' Sophie said.

'Instead of a couple of days you've provided
yourself with luxury board and lodging for a whole
week.'

About to reply with an indignant protest, she took
a breath and counted to ten. Slowly. So he remained
hostile, but so what? No matter how annoying and
frustrating this might be, she had achieved her
objective in coming to Germany in that Rudy's
admittance into the von Lössingen household was
now a *fait accompli*.

'The only reason I'm staying here,' she told him,
'is because Frau von Lössingen has asked me to. She
asked because she intends to do her best for Rudy,
and that's because she accepts I'm telling the truth

and he is your brother's child,' Sophie announced, shining him a smile which hollered 'so there'.

'Maybe she does,' Diether replied coolly. 'However, a word of advice — don't think you have this all sewn up. As soon as the Italians leave I shall be making enquiries to authenticate your story, and should authentication not be forthcoming——' He spread his hands.

CHAPTER THREE

HELENE VON LÖSSINGEN plucked at the flounces which decorated the neckline of her turquoise cocktail dress, then lifted her coat and jet-beaded evening bag from the sofa.

'I feel so bad about leaving you to baby-sit,' she said. 'If it had been possible I would've cancelled this evening, but I'm chairperson of the committee which has organised the dinner.'

Sophie smiled. 'I don't mind,' she said.

'I'd have asked Marie to look after Rudy, but it's her night off and she has something planned which can't easily be changed.'

'I'm fine,' she insisted.

'But Diether's entertaining his Italians again and Axel's going to the cinema with a girlfriend, so you'll be all on your own,' Helene fretted.

'And perfectly content,' Sophie assured her, a mite wearily.

All day the older woman had been apologising for the long-standing engagement and spouting regrets about her absence, and all day she had been telling her—with sincerity—that she was happy to stay in with the baby.

'You will help yourself to some supper?' Helene said, as she put on her fur coat. 'There's *Kartoffel-salat mit Würstcher* in the fridge and *Käse*, or if you prefer——'

'I shan't starve,' she protested. 'Please, go and enjoy yourself.'

As the noise of the car faded away down the drive, Sophie laid back her head and closed her eyes. Her hostess was a likeable, warm-hearted woman, but after two days continually in her company she was more than ready for a break. When Diether had warned that his stepmother fussed and spoiled, he had been right. The fussing meant that not a single item—be it a baby-bath, shampoo or disposable napkins—had been bought without endless discussion; that umpteen anxious enquiries had turned her explanation of Rudy's diet into a three-hour event; that Helene had insisted on making a same-day appointment with her doctor to check whether the baby's innoculations were in line with German requirements. And as for spoiling—Sophie sighed. If Rudy made one murmur, he was immediately picked up and cuddled. Right now he did not seem too thrilled by this, yet in a couple of months' time he could be expecting—and demanding—instant attention. As tactfully as she could, she had pointed out the problems which might be being created and yet, although Helen had agreed that her remarks made sense, nothing had changed. A squeak, and she rushed to pet him.

Sophie gave a wry smile. What it needed was for Diether to issue the warning, *then* it would be taken seriously. His stepmother might have insisted on welcoming in her and Rudy, but it had quickly become apparent that such independence was an aberration and that in everything else she referred to, and deferred to Diether. He was the boss, the puppet master who pulled her strings. One word

from him, and Helene — and Axel, for that matter —
jumped to do his bidding. Though Diether did not
string-pull in any obstreperous way. He diffidently
and engagingly and politely suggested, and it was
done.

His manner towards her was now polite, too,
Sophie reflected. Their contact over the past two
days might have been brief, yet he had had the
opportunity to resume his attack. He did not. When
they had met on the stairs, or he had joined her and
Helene to watch the early evening news, Diether's
courtesy had been impeccable. Yet threaded
through it was a steely strand which advised he did
not approve of her presence, and that she and Rudy
remained on sufferance.

Abruptly Sophie opened her eyes, alerted by the
sound of footsteps in the hall to the fact that her
censor was now on his way out, too. Sitting upright,
she reached for the door-stop-sized paperback which
she had bought at the airport. Whatever his attitude
he would *not* be allowed to faze her.

Obviously fresh from the shower, and with his jaw
newly shaved, and wearing a smart navy pin-stripe
suit, Diether strolled into the room. He looked every
inch the urbane man-about-town.

'I've no doubt Helene'll have made sure you've
been provided with every last thing you could possibly require while you're baby-sitting,' he remarked
drily.

Sophie's eyes met his in a crystal-cool look. 'Yes,
you need have no fears. My solitary evening will be
spent in unbridled comfort.'

'Your evening isn't going to be solitary,' he said.

Alarm twisted in her stomach. Did this mean that,

despite the debonair appearance, his arrangements had fallen through and she was to have his company? And if so, could he be intending to dispense with the veneer of politeness and use the next three hours for a concentrated bout of verbal pummelling?

'Why not?' Sophie asked warily.

'Because Axel'll be with you.'

'I thought he had a date,' she protested.

'He's cancelled it.'

She shot him a suspicious look. While it was a relief to know she would not be heckled, what was the reason for this change of plan? Had the young man decided he did not want to go out, or could Diether have realised that even the maid would be absent and given instructions that she was not to be left alone in the house? The von Lössingens were wealthy and it showed—in the antique furniture which filled the rooms, in the displays of enamelled snuff-boxes, in the diamond rings and other jewellery which Helene wore, and doubtless kept in a velvet box upstairs. She bridled. Not only did he consider her a liar and an opportunist, it seemed he also suspected she might well be a thief!

'Axel's keeping guard?' she enquired stiffly.

Diether gave a cold flash of a smile. 'I would've thought it unlikely that anyone would break in and rape you, but I guess you could make that interpretation.'

'I didn't mean guarding me, I meant guarding the——' Sophie started but stopped, her words ending in an invisible cul-de-sac as she realised he could have deliberately misunderstood and was baiting her. 'I shall enjoy making up a twosome with Axel,' she informed him, her chin tilting.

'And I'll enjoy making up a twosome with you,' Axel said, hearing what she had said as he loped in through the door.

Diether bade her a civil goodbye, but as he went out his brother followed, telling him about a camping trip which a couple of his friends had proposed and how keen he was to take part.

Left alone, Sophie frowned. She could understand a little wariness of this stranger who had produced a von Lössingen heir out of thin air, but Diether was downright distrustful—and she seemed to be stuck with the reputation of bad girl! Her frown deepened. Although, initially, she had decided she would ignore the threat which he had left hanging the other day, it had become clear that she could ill afford to do so. Her mission was *not* accomplished. Helene might insist the baby belonged with her, but there could now be little doubt that should her stepson decide to order his deportation she would give way. Not without a protest, but ultimately. Diether's enquiries must produce something tangible, she mused—such as a bank record of the transfer of the five thousand pounds—yet would he regard that as sufficient authentication? Sophie straightened her spine. Nothing worthwhile was said to be easy, so she would regard his attitude as a challenge and do her best to win him over. She did not know how, but he *had* to be won over, because otherwise Rudy's future would never be secure.

With a sigh, she opened her book and found her place. One page had been read and she was about to start on the next when Axel came back in.

'Diether's happy for me to go on the camping

holiday,' he told her cheerily, dropping down at the other end of the sofa.

'How generous of him,' Sophie muttered in German, for when his brother was not around both the young man and his mother spoke in their own language with her. 'Diether appears to play the dominant role here,' she could not resist saying, a touch sharply.

Axel shrugged. '*Ja.*'

'You don't mind?'

He gave a reflective smile. 'We've had some savage battles in our time, but no. After all, if it weren't for him we wouldn't *be* here.'

'What do you mean?' Sophie asked curiously.

'We wouldn't be living in this house, nor be able to enjoy such a pleasant lifestyle. You see, before he died my father suffered several years of ill health when he withdrew into himself and showed very little interest in the business——' Axel grimaced '—or in us kids. So when he dropped off his perch ten years ago,' he continued irreverently, 'the Von Lössingen company was on the brink of bankruptcy.'

Sophie visualised the affluent and thriving works complex which she had visited. 'Bankruptcy?' she protested.

The youth nodded. 'Dad was a proud man and he'd gone to great pains to conceal how dire the situation actually was, but when he died and the truth was revealed——' He rolled his eyes. 'The order book was almost empty and the only reason the firm had continued to function was thanks to funding by two banks. However, they threatened to foreclose and it seemed as though my mother would be forced to sell everything in order to pay them off, but Diether negotiated a holding arrangement, took charge of the company and started to drum up trade.'

She frowned. 'How old was he then?'

'Twenty-seven.'

'The same age as I am now,' Sophie murmured, thinking that it must have demanded courage for such a young man to have taken on that kind of a burden.

'Because he'd done an engineering degree and then spent time in the States studying for a business qualification, he'd had minimal work experience, but he built up the company all over again, though better because it was never as big nor as prosperous under Dad as it is now,' Axel continued, exhibiting a strong streak of hero-worship. 'For years Diether worked sixteen hours a day, and travelled the world trying to secure orders, so you see it's thanks to him we survived.' The latter part of his account had been exuberant, but now he sighed. 'It's such a shame that Johannes didn't, nor Christa.'

'Christa?' Sophie queried.

'Diether's wife.'

'He's been married?' she said, in surprise.

'Yes, but he was really broken up when Christa died and even now, five years later, he hates it if anyone refers to it. Diether keeps himself emotionally to himself, though I suppose that's because his memories are too painful. They'd lived together for a while and then decided to get married,' Axel explained, 'but a few months later Christa was dead.'

'What did she die of?' Sophie asked.

'A rare illness. It has a long name.' He screwed

up his face. 'I can't remember it. But let's talk about you,' he said, moving towards her along the sofa. 'Do you have a boyfriend?'

'There's someone I go out with in London,' she said, thinking of the amiable but uninspiring young man she was currently dating, 'but——'

'It's not serious?'

'No.'

'So you're available?'

Sophie smiled at the phrase. 'You could say that.'

'What kind of men turn you on?' Axel enquired. 'Tall, blond, sexy ones?'

She shot him a startled look. He was describing Diether. As if in reflex, her mind travelled back to the first time his dark blue eyes had met hers and something had stirred inside her. She also recalled how he had loosened his tie the other evening and the gesture had seemed so attractive. Sophie frowned. She was having a brainstorm. Diether von Lössingen might pack an undeniable sexual punch, but he did not appeal to her! She was just about to advise her questioner that his big brother left her cold—ice-cold—when she recognised from the slightly smug curl of his mouth that he was referring to himself. She stared in surprise. While Axel was admittedly strapping and blond, she did not consider he possessed much in the way of sex appeal. Girls around his own age might swoon but, at roughly five years her junior, he ranked in her mind as no more than a pretty choirboy.

'Um—I've nothing against blond men,' Sophie began, wondering how she could clearly, yet tact-fully let him know she did not find him an Adonis.

'Great!' Axel said, with relish.

She frowned, and felt the first flicker of panic as she realised just how close he was sitting. Indeed, if Axel inched any nearer along the sofa, he would have her fastened into the corner. By saying she would enjoy making up a twosome, she appeared to have given him entirely the wrong impression.

'However, I'm not interested in — um — any kind of — um — an involvement,' she continued stiltedly.

The young man smiled, apparently deciding she was now playing hard to get. 'Then I'll need to persuade you,' he said, and put his hand on her knee.

Sophie froze. Last year she had been the unwilling target of an ardently pursuing male, and now a feeling of *déjà vu* took hold and the old sensations of fear and entrapment rose up like bile in her throat.

'I'm not interested!' she repeated fiercely, and knocked his hand away.

Axel blinked, looking both surprised by her vehemence and contrite. 'I'm sorry,' he said. 'I never intended to — '

'It's OK,' Sophie cut in, and shone a hasty smile. She had misjudged, over-reacted. Before her pursuer had been a devious and calculating married man, whereas Axel was merely a youth making experimental advances. 'I'm only here for a week,' she muttered, needing to offer some kind of an excuse and mollification.

'Yes, but — ' He stopped as the telephone rang in the hall and, with a sigh, went out to answer it. 'Someone for you,' he reported, coming back a minute or two later.

'It's me — Eva,' a voice said in German, when

Sophie lifted the receiver. 'How're you getting along?'

She grimaced. 'Things aren't perfect, but I'll tell you all about it when I see you on Monday.'

'That's why I'm ringing — to ask if we can get together before then. On Thursday evening Giles and I are going to a *Karneval* dinner and dance at one of Cologne's premier hotels,' she explained, 'and we wondered if you could join us? I know it's short notice, but you'd enjoy it,' Eva appealed.

Sophie frowned. It would be good to sample the *Karneval* celebrations which, she knew, got under way in Germany before Christmas and ended at the start of Lent, yet she hesitated. Although Helene had said that, after tonight, she would be in every evening until her departure, she had overheard her on the phone telling someone that if they were desperate maybe she could make up a four for bridge on Thursday evening. In which event, the maid would be left in charge of Rudy.

'I'm not sure what's happening here,' she replied, 'so can I get back to you in the morning?'

'No problem,' her friend assured her.

Returning to the drawing-room, she found Axel sprawled in an armchair watching television. When he next spoke his manner was casual and for the remainder of the evening the young Lothario made no more provocative comments. He had got the message, Sophie decided thankfully.

Some time in the middle of the night distant wails intruded into her consciousness, and it penetrated that Rudy was crying. For a while Sophie drifted, not quite falling asleep again and yet not coming properly awake, but his cries continued. Stretching out an arm, she fumbled for the switch on the bedside lamp and peered at the dial on her travelling alarm. It was three a.m. Helene must have come home long ago, so why hadn't she gone to him? As the wails grew louder, she sighed and pushed back the sheet. Diether would not appreciate being awoken in the small hours, she thought wryly, so she had better quieten Rudy, and fast.

Barefoot, she crept surrepititiously along the carpeted landing and into the baby's room.

'Oh, no,' Sophie sighed, when she saw the reason for his cries.

Before going to bed, she had checked him and then Rudy had been asleep in his cot alone. However, on her return home his grandmother must have peeped in and decided he needed company, for now the baby kicked and squealed among a multitude of soft toys, the largest of which—an almost toddler-size teddy bear—had fallen on top of him. Removing the bear and all the other intruders, Sophie laid the sobbing child against her shoulder.

'Did you get a shock?' she murmured, gently rocking him. 'Never mind, you're all right now.'

Gradually his sobs lessened into snuffles, the snuffles became yawns, and not much later she laid him down. In minutes, he was asleep again.

Leaving his room, Sophie tiptoed past her door and headed down the stairs. She needed a drink, but there was no glass in her bathroom. In the kitchen, she switched on the light and began opening cupboards. Where were the tumblers? Oops! A pile of plastic bowls which had been untidily stacked tumbled out and bounced, scattering every which

way on the polished terracotta tiled floor. Quickly
gathering them up, Sophie replaced them. She had
resumed her search, when upstairs one muted click
followed by another warned that a door had opened
and closed. Tilting her head to listen, she heard the
occasional creak of someone stealthily making his or
her way downstairs. Her heart sank. Had Axel also
been disturbed by the baby, heard her come down
and decided to follow? Was his amorous pursuit to
be continued after all? The young man might hesi-
tate to invade the privacy of her bedroom, but he
could regard the kitchen as common ground.

Darting over, Sophie doused the light. If Axel
found the room in darkness, he would decide she
had gone back to bed and retreat. As the footsteps
padded across the hall, she tucked herself into a
space at the far end of a length of pine units, and
waited. The footsteps came nearer until, peeping
out sideways through the shadows, she saw the door
open. Rearing back, Sophie stood as still as a statue.
Go away, she urged silently. Go away! But, a
moment later, the light was snapped on. Dazzled by
the glare, she blinked, then gawked in surprise as
Diether prowled like a cautious tiger into the middle
of the kitchen. His shirt was unbuttoned and hung
free of his trousers, and he wore socks but no shoes.
He had obviously been in the middle of undressing
when he had come down.

Scanning the large room, he slowly began to
swivel, but before his gaze had time to reach her
Sophie stepped forward.

'Hello,' she said.

Diether jumped, muttering something in German

which she did not understand, but which sounded like an obscenity.

'You must've had a late night,' she remarked.

'Too late,' he muttered. His brow furrowed. 'What the hell are you doing?'

'I came to get myself a glass of water.'

'In the dark?' he protested. 'I heard noises and——'

'Straight away decided I must be filching the silver?' Sophie interrupted. Standing erect, she flung wide her arms. 'Sorry to disappoint, but as you can see I'm empty-handed.'

'Yes, you'd have difficulty concealing anything in that outfit,' Diether observed drily.

Hot colour flooded her cheeks. In her rush to attend to the baby she had not bothered with her robe, and the lilac nightdress she wore was a clingy, shoe-string-strapped, low-cut affair. Made of silk and inset with an arrowed panel of lace which, beneath his gaze, began to feel as if it was transparent, the garment tended to be revealing at the best of times. But her defiant stance, which had tautened her breasts and emphasised their creamy swell in the brief bodice, had made the nightdress downright risqué.

'I *did* come for a drink,' Sophie gabbled, dropping her arms and fighting the urge to fling them protectively across her chest, 'but I thought you were Axel and that you'd heard me come downstairs and were following me. And I thought that if I switched off the light he would decide he'd made a mistake.'

It appeared to require an effort before Diether could drag his eyes back to her face. 'Why should you think Axel would follow you?' he enquired.

'I shouldn't, and he didn't. I made a mistake, but—well, this evening he was coming on to me and—and I'm sensitive about such things.'

He frowned, plainly bewildered by her explanation but disinclined to pursue it. 'As Axel sleeps like the proverbial log, I can guarantee he wouldn't have heard you—nor that volley of bumps.'

'Some plastic bowls fell on to the floor when I was looking for a glass,' Sophie explained.

'I see. And did you get your drink?' Diether enquired.

'Not yet.'

He went to a cupboard which she had failed to investigate and took out two tumblers. 'I'll join you. Did you particularly want water, or would you like something else?' he asked, opening the fridge. 'I'm having a cola.'

'I'll have one, too. Thanks,' she said, when he handed her a brimming glass.

Diether drank a couple of mouthfuls, then rested a lean hip against the kitchen table. 'From the photographs of Lisette I got the impression that she's what used to be called a hippy,' he said.

'I suppose so,' Sophie agreed. 'She's an airy-fairy character who appears to have spent most of her adult life on the move, taking whatever work she can and living where she can. Though she's not very adult. She may be twenty, but it's twenty going on fifteen.'

'How did she come to live with you?' he enquired.

'I was renting out a room and Lisette answered my advertisement in the newsagent's window,' she explained.

'You were short of cash?'

Sophie sighed. His question sounded like an accusation *and* a condemnation.

'I rented out the room because I needed a little extra, but I wasn't destitute. My grandfather died last year and left me a small terraced house in London, and I've been modernising and repainting the place with the intention of selling it,' she told him. 'And that takes money.'

Diether frowned and, pushing a hand inside his shirt, began to rub at the whorls of golden hair which curled on his chest. 'Why did your friend decide to go to America?' he enquired.

'She'd met some people who were planning to wander around the southern states and they suggested she join them. You call Lisette a friend, but she wasn't,' Sophie went on. 'We liked each other well enough, but our personalities were too different for us to share an affinity. And although my house was her base she didn't spend that much time there.'

'Where did she spend it?'

'Some days she helped out on a market stall and some evenings she worked in a bar, though there was no apparent routine. And in between she hung around with a group of contemporaries who didn't have full-time jobs either.'

'Did she take the baby with her?'

'To start with, yes, but then I looked after him. You see, Lisette alternated between treating him as if he were a doll or neglecting him, and I couldn't let that happen.' Sophie sighed. 'If I'd realised I was going to end up being a surrogate mother, if I'd known she *had* a baby, I would never have rented her the room.'

'She didn't tell you about Rudy?'

'No. The first time I realised he existed was when he was released from hospital a couple of weeks later and she suddenly produced him.'

Diether continued to rub at his chest. 'So if Lisette didn't tell you the truth about that she might not have been telling the truth about Johannes being the baby's father or about the money he's supposed to have sent her either.'

Sophie gave an impatient sigh. 'She didn't admit to having a baby because the room was really too small for her to have one there, and she realised that if she'd told me about him I would never have agreed. She admitted that afterwards. But why should she lie about Johannes or the money?'

'People tell lies for a multitude of reasons,' Diether remarked, fixing her with piercing blue eyes.

'Maybe,' she said, refusing to react to what seemed to be a thrust against her, 'but omitting to mention something is different from deliberately constructing a pretence, and I can assure you that Lisette didn't have the ingenuity to sustain a lie for months without arousing my suspicions.' She took a sip from her glass. 'You said she abandoned Rudy because she didn't care, but I'm sure it was because she felt inadequate.'

'Inadequate?'

Sophie nodded. 'At first I put her attitude towards Rudy down to his spending the first months of his life in hospital and her failing to bond, but then I realised the problem was Lisette's lack of maturity. She hadn't grown up enough emotionally to be able to take charge of another human being. She'd obtained a passport for Rudy, so I assume that originally she'd intended to take him with her to

America, only she'd recognised that it wouldn't be in his best interests. You see, in her note Lisette said Rudy had always felt like a weight dragging her down and that he'd be much better off with me.' She sighed. 'Unfortunately she hadn't thought it through properly and realised that I wouldn't be allowed, or in a position, to keep him.'

'And her lack of maturity is why you're so sure she won't suddenly reappear and want him back?'

'Yes. Looking after him terrifies her.'

His hand abstractedly massaging, Diether regarded her in silence. Sophie wished he would keep still. He had dishevelled and opened his shirt, and her eyes were drawn to the contours of the muscular chest which tapered into a trim waist. As if mesmerised, she watched the rhythmic, circling motion. The hair would feel coarse beneath his fingertips, the bronzed skin smooth. Was he tanned all over? she wondered. Germans often exhibited a confident approach towards nudity, so did his Caribbean tan extend from head to toe or was there a thin band of white around his thighs? Abruptly, she realised that his eyes had fallen to her breasts. Sophie's cheeks flamed. Her interest in his body had invoked an unconscious physical response in her own, for her nipples had tautened to lift the fine silk of her nightdress. Raising her glass to her lips, she gulped down the cola. So much for Diether leaving her cold!

'Earlier Helene had put the big teddy bear she bought for Rudy in his cot,' she said.

He blinked. 'Sorry?'

'The bear was in his cot, and it toppled on top of him and made him cry. Do you think you could have a word and suggest he doesn't need all those toys in with him?'

'I'd have said he doesn't need all those toys, period,' Diether remarked, and drained his glass. 'I'll speak to her.'

'Thanks, and could you also ask if she'd refrain from trying to force-feed him? I've explained that Rudy's gaining weight and in another few months or so will catch up with his contemporaries, but she seems to think that because he's small he has to be continually stuffed full of food.'

'OK.'

'And——'

'Could this wait?' he appealed wearily. 'It is the middle of the night, and I would appreciate at least a couple of hours' sleep before I'm plunged into the next round of negotiations.'

'Sorry,' Sophie said. 'How're things going?' she asked, as they walked out into the hall.

Diether grimaced. 'At the moment everything's stalled while we haggle over costs. What's needed is some kind of a push.' He lifted a brow. 'You wouldn't be willing to come and tap-dance on the table?'

'And be a party to bribery? Not a chance,' she said smartly, then frowned. 'My friends in Bonn have invited me to a dinner on Thursday——'

'So?' he enquired, when she paused.

'I don't know whether I should accept. You see, if I go and if Helene's invited to play bridge, she'll leave Rudy with Marie.'

'You don't think that's a good idea?'

Sophie shook her head. 'Marie may be an excellent cook, but she's—well, nervous and indecisive, and if there was some kind of an emergency she could panic.'

'Do you want me to tell Helene she's not to leave him?' Diether asked.

'Please, and, for the future, I think she should employ a nanny. Helene obviously leads a busy life and you were correct — she's not going to want to cut down on her activities — and until Rudy's older he needs proper care.'

He came to a halt at the foot of the stairs and faced her. 'You're offering your services?'

'Pardon me?'

'Do you intend to be the nanny? Is this why you came?' he demanded, his eyes suddenly ablaze with fury. 'You've established a friendship with my stepmother, gone all out to ingratiate yourself, and now you think she'll pay over the odds to secure you?'

Sophie glared. 'I have *not* tried to ingratiate myself, neither do I have a pound sign flashing over my head, and, as difficult as you may find this to believe, I don't want the damn job!'

'Keep your voice down, you'll waken everyone,' Diether protested, then his brow creased. 'You don't?'

'Not on your life,' she spat. 'But I do think it would be preferable if Helene hires someone as soon as possible, because I'm unhappy about the prospect of Rudy being left with Marie.'

His anger evaporated as quickly as it had arisen. 'I'll mention it,' he said tiredly.

'Thank you.' Sophie hesitated. 'You think Rudy'll be all right with Helene on Thursday evening?'

'Why not?' Diether enquired, setting off up the

stairs. 'She looked after Johannes and Axel when they were small.'

'Yes, but——'

He made a curt sound of impatience. 'Just ring your friend and tell her you'll go,' he said, speaking over his shoulder.

Sophie trudged after him. 'OK, I will.'

CHAPTER FOUR

SOPHIE stood with Rudy at the drawing-room window.

'That,' she informed him, with a gesture outside, 'is called snow.'

It was Thursday afternoon, and the snowy weather which had long been predicted had finally arrived. At noon fat flakes had begun drifting down from the sky; they had fallen constantly and were still falling, and now the world was covered in a blanket of white. Sophie frowned. If the snow continued it could make travelling hazardous, and in half an hour's time she was due to set off for Bonn.

As she gazed out at the Christmas-card scene, there was the soft swoosh of tyres and a silver top-of-the-range Mercedes sports car swung off the road and up the drive. Her brown-green eyes widened. Diether had come home, but why so early? She watched him climb out of the vehicle, tug up the collar of his black leather coat, and, with long strides, begin to make his way across the front of the house. His head was bent against the falling snow, but as he reached the window he suddenly glanced up, stopped, and wiggled his fingers at the baby. Unprepared for such a playful gesture, Sophie gawked at him, then she raised Rudy's arm.

'Wave,' she instructed, and he chuckled and bobbed excitedly up and down. 'Rudy's taken a shine to you,' she remarked a minute or two later when Diether came into the room and the baby continued to crow. 'All day he's been serious, but you appear and—hey presto!—smiles.'

Diether had shed his coat, and now he bent his head and began to brush errant flakes of snow out of his hair. 'You're going for the emotional jugular,' he said, though his tone was wry, rather than condemning.

'Would you like to hold him?' Sophie suggested, as Rudy craned towards him.

'No,' he said, the word terse.

'He doesn't bite,' she protested.

'No, thank you,' Diether repeated, straightening.

Sophie stared. 'What's happened to your tie?' she asked, for all he wore around his neck was a knot from which hung a couple of fraying inches of navy polka-dotted silk.

'It's been cut off.'

'So I see, but why?'

'Because today is *Weiberfastnacht*—Ladies' Day. It's the day during *Karneval* when the fairer sex live it up a little and let loose,' he explained. 'I believe it's a throw-back to the times when women were subdued, a notion which——' he arched a brow '—is outside your area of experience.'

'And cutting off ties is part of the letting loose?' Sophie enquired.

Diether nodded. 'They're regarded as trophies and the idea is to gather as many as possible, so when I arrived at the office this morning I was set upon by a gang of females, each wielding a pair of scissors. They were so damned eager that, for a minute or two, I was afraid they might get carried away and chop off some other, more personal part of me by mistake,' he said, and gave a descriptively agonised grin. 'However, I'm relieved to report that I came through intact.' He flapped the castrated tie. 'More or less.'

She studied him. Her initial reaction was surprise that his staff should feel so at ease that they could approach him in such a way, but today Diether von Lössingen seemed eminently approachable. Though he probably always was, Sophie thought — with other people. Yet even the guarded and critical air he usually displayed towards her had disappeared, and he brimmed with good humour.

'You've worked out a deal with the Italians,' she said, hoisting the baby higher up in her arms.

'An extremely worthwhile deal.' His deep blue eyes shone and he beamed. For a moment he looked tempted to gather her and Rudy up in a hug, but instead he pushed his hands into his trouser pockets and rocked contentedly back on his heels. 'The costings are all agreed, so now it's just a matter of the legal guys doing a final check before the contract's typed out, ready for the formal signing before Signor Angellino and his merry men fly back to Milan in the morning.'

Sophie grinned. 'Congratulations.'

'Thanks,' he said, with a smile.

'Helene told me you'd had to fight off some stiff competition before they'd agree to sit down at the table; how did you do that?' she asked.

'By being more determined and presenting a slick case. First of all, we had a video made, in Italian, which detailed all the advantages of them having their car components made in our factory. Then we——'

Diether talked on, enthusiastically detailing how the deal had gradually come about.

'Am I missing something?' Helene enquired, when she walked in to hear him buoyant and reminiscent a few minutes later.

'The Italians have agreed terms,' he told her.

'*Wunderbar!*' she exclaimed, and reached up to kiss him on both cheeks. 'Surely this calls for champagne?'

'It does,' he agreed, 'but not now. At least, not for me. I'm socialising again this evening and, while it's not for a few hours, I'll be driving, and in view of the weather I'd prefer to remain stone-cold sober.'

Helene cast an anxious look out through the window. 'What state are the roads in?' she asked.

'The minor ones are covered in snow, but the main ones are clear — so far.'

'But if I go slowly on the hill I should be all right? I'm just about to run Sophie down to the station,' she explained.

'I'll do it,' Diether said promptly. He turned to her. 'I'll take you to your friends' house.'

'Thanks, but there's no need,' Sophie protested. 'If you drop me at the station here, I can get a taxi when I reach Bonn. I have directions and apparently it's only a fifteen-minute drive.'

'But everyone'll be wanting taxis in this weather and there may not be any,' Helene said worriedly.

'So I'll take you,' Diether repeated, in a tone which deterred any further argument. 'Are you ready to go?'

'Almost. I'll just put Rudy down for a sleep, then I'll be with you.'

After staying awake for most of the day the baby had looked drowsy, but when Sophie laid him in his cot he started to cry. Reluctant to relinquish him to Helen's fussing, she rocked and soothed and eventually managed to settle him, but this took time, and it was three-quarters of an hour later before she walked with Diether out to his car. By now it was dark.

'I'm sorry I've kept you waiting,' Sophie apologised, as she buckled herself into the front seat beside him. 'Rudy seemed fretful.' She frowned. 'I do hope he's going to be all right.'

'You're the one who's fretful,' Diether told her, turning the key in the ignition. 'He'll be fine.'

She sighed. He was right.

'It's good of you to act as chauffeur, but,' she added pertly, 'aren't you getting a little slack?'

'Slack?' he queried.

'Aren't you frightened of encouraging me with acts of kindness?'

He angled her a mocking glance. 'You've got it wrong. This isn't an act of kindness. This is me taking the opportunity to see what sort of place your friends live in and to gauge the kind of people they are,' he said blightingly, and reversed down the drive and out on to the road.

Sophie gripped the seatbelt in a strangle-hold. She had decided that, somewhere among his good mood, a lessening of hostilities could be detected, but the put-down made it clear that she had been incredibly, pathetically, irritatingly naïve.

'According to Eva, she and Giles live in a most attractive house,' she declared, and paused to shine a buttoned-up, disdainful smile. 'But then diplomatic families often do.'

Diether's head jerked round in surprise. 'The guy is a diplomat?'

'A British one — though Eva, his wife, is German.'

Frowning, he moved into second gear and the Mercedes surged forward. 'How long have you known them?'

'Seven years. After I left college, my first job was caring for their daughters. They have three and, at that time, the girls were aged one, two and three.'

'It must've been hard work.'

'Life was hectic,' Sophie agreed, her anger beginning to subside as she recalled hustle-bustle moments from the past, 'but it was also happy. Because both Giles and Eva are easygoing, the employer–employee relationship quickly became that of friends. Eva's the vivacious type and she saw no reason why having three kids in as many years should cramp her style,' she went on, 'so there were lots of outings, regular skiing trips, frequent visits to her parents who live in Hamburg. Giles wasn't always able to go along, but, of course, I did.'

'You worked for them in London?' Diether enquired, negotiating a corner and heading downhill.

'Yes, for three years — until Giles received a posting to Singapore. They were keen for me to go with them, but I decided the time had come for a change. However, via letters and phone calls and visits when they come on home leave, our friendship has continued. Last year Giles was posted to Bonn, and when I rang to ask if Rudy and I could stay they were delighted.'

'If you were so happy with them, why decide to make a change?' he questioned.

'Because I was becoming too attached to the girls. Becoming too fond of my charges is one of my failings,' Sophie said, her brown-green eyes clouding as she thought of how fond she had become of Rudy. 'I know that the *Karneval* festivities differ in different parts of Germany, but what form do they take here?' she asked, needing a diversion.

'In the main, there are dances, parties and costume balls,' Diether told her. 'As the months go by, the excitement builds until in the last week, which is this week, it reaches fever pitch. Then there are processions, and——'

'I noticed clown-shaped cakes when I was out shopping with Helene,' she cut in.

He nodded. 'Clowns are a feature. However, on Monday it's *Rosenmontag*—Rose Monday,' he translated, 'which is the day before Shrove Tuesday, and that's when people dress up in all kinds of costumes——' he lifted a hand from the wheel '—and march with bands in the final parade. One of the best and most famous parades is held in Cologne. You're moving on to your friends on Monday, so you should ask them to take you to see it. It's good fun.'

They had reached the foot of the hill and, as they turned north along the banks of the Rhine, the highway which stretched ahead was snow-free. Diether had been restricting his speed, but now he accelerated. The parade may be fun, Sophie brooded, as the car began to eat up the miles, but she did not find the prospect of staying in Bonn so amusing. As fond as she was of Eva and Giles and their family, given the choice she would have said goodbye to Rudy and taken the first flight home; for so long as she remained in the vicinity there would be the constant temptation to go and see the baby again, for one last time. She bit deep into her lip. But a visit had been agreed and was expected of her.

Yet did there have to be one last time? Sophie mused. Not necessarily. Later in the year, she could come to Germany again and check on Rudy's progress — briefly, so that he was not unsettled. Though, she reflected, it was possible that by then he would have forgotten all about her. She frowned. She was getting ahead of herself and taking too much for granted. With the Italian deal out of the way, Diether would be attempting to authenticate her story — and if he could not do so to his satisfaction then she would be summoned to take the baby away. Maybe this month, maybe next. . .

'Did you know that Beethoven was born here and lived here?' Diether enquired.

'No,' she said, realising from the government buildings and diplomatic missions which ranged on either side of the road that they must have reached Bonn.

'The *Beethoven-Haus* is in the centre of town, in the pedestrianised area. It's open to the public and well worth a visit.'

'Hasn't Bonn always been the capital?' Sophie asked, deciding she would rather talk than brood.

'No, just since 1949, but now, in addition to the *Bundestag* and scores of government departments, there are one hundred and twenty-three embassies. It's a good place to live,' Diether went on. 'The many parks make the city green and it's in a beautiful setting. There's the river—the promenade is the longest on the Rhine—and the hills, and——'

Sophie was still smarting from having been so comprehensively snubbed earlier, and now she saw a chance to retaliate and punish him a little.

'I understand an American once described Bonn as half the size of a Chicago cemetery and twice as dead,' Sophie remarked coolly.

'Compared with political centres like London and Washington, Bonn is tiny, and if you want to live among millions it can't compete,' he acknowledged, unperturbed, 'but dead? Never. As well as the energy provided by the mix of nationalities, there's a thriving university which means the town is full of young people. There are theatres and concert halls,' he continued, sounding like someone from the tourist board, 'and an art museum, plus——'

Diether's song of praise lasted until they reached the *Kennedybrücke*, the bridge over the Rhine which had been named in honour of President Kennedy. Now he required directions, and Sophie acted as navigator, taking them away from the city and out into the countryside. After a few miles they reached a village, where they turned into a residential area of prosperous detached dwellings and elegant streets lined with silver birch.

'That's Eva's house,' she said, seeing the number on a low white modern villa which was half hidden behind a thick hedge of fir.

Diether parked and as he went round to the boot to get her suitcase she clambered out.

'Thank you for the lift,' Sophie was saying, as she made her way to the back of the car, but all of a sudden her foot slipped on the snow-covered pavement and she started to slide. 'Aarrgh!' she gasped, arms flailing.

Diether looked round, straightened and, as she skidded towards the kerb, lurched forward. Wham! Sophie crashed into him. He gave a startled laugh and grabbed her, holding her upright.

'Are you all right?' he asked.

'Y—yes,' she said, winded by the impact and trying to catch her breath.

He grinned. 'For a moment there, I thought you were going to knock me flat.'

'Y—yes,' Sophie said again.

She was held close in his arms, close against his chest, and her already galloping heart broke into a wild rhythm. The embrace might be just an automatic response to save her, yet it seemed alarmingly intimate—and she was aware of them frozen in a lovers' tableau. Diether was standing on the road while she remained on the pavement, and the difference in height had brought them almost level. Sophie gazed at him. The light from a streetlamp edged his cheekbones and the strong line of his jaw in black shadow, while, at the same time, it had gilded his hair into a burnished helmet of gold. He reminded her of an ethereal blond god. A god full of intoxicating allure.

'Eat it,' he murmured.

'What?' she said, startled.

When Diether raised his hand and gently touched her lips with a long finger, Sophie's nerves jangled. A tremor ran through her body. This violation of her personal space seemed so erotic that she found it difficult to keep still.

'There's a snowflake,' he said.

'Oh.' Putting out the pink tip of her tongue, she traced slowly around the edges of her mouth until she felt the soft fragment of ice, then she licked it away. 'OK now?' she enquired breathlessly.

'OK,' Diether replied, and he released her, lifted her suitcase from the boot and slammed down the lid.

At the noise, Sophie snapped back to life. What a fool! she thought, berating herself. She had been melting inside and moonstruck, while all the time he was matter-of-fact.

Suddenly, the porch light of the house was switched on and the front door opened.

'Sophie!' a voice cried, and she turned to see a slender, pretty woman excitedly waving. Her copper-coloured hair was cut in a short smooth bob, and she wore a casual black top and leggings.

'Don't come out,' Sophie called, for Eva seemed all set to bound down through the snow to greet her. 'I'll be back before noon tomorrow,' she rattled off at Diether, and reached for her case. 'Bye.'

'I'll carry it to the door for you,' he said, firmly taking hold.

'But——'

'You might skid again,' he said, and, gesturing that she should go first, he followed her up the path.

Eva welcomed her warmly, then eyed Diether with undisguised interest.

'*Guten Abend*,' she said, with a smile.

'Good evening,' he replied.

'Eva, this is Diether von Lössingen. Diether, meet Eva Thompson,' Sophie said, in a crisp, short introduction.

'I thought your car looked rather splendid to be a

taxi and that you were too special for a driver,' the redhead told him, as they formally shook hands. 'Come in and have a drink.'

Diether grinned. 'That's very kind of —'

'You can't,' Sophie rushed in, before he could get any further. 'You're driving.'

'Respectable' was written over the neighbour-hood, over the house, and over her friend in capital letters, so she saw no reason for him to come inside. Yet it was not so much the thought of him asking questions and making an assessment which she objected to, but his physical presence. By holding her, Diether had unsettled her and until he had departed her equipoise would remain in tatters.

'The drink doesn't need to be alcoholic,' Eva said. 'I can easily make coffee.'

Diether shot Sophie a glance. 'Well. . .' he said, languidly drawing out the word.

Her fingers bunched into tight balls of tension. Go, go, *go*, she ordered, wishing she could grab hold of his collar and frog-march him down to the Mercedes.

'I'll take a rain-check if I may,' he completed, after minutes, hours, what seemed like days had gone by. 'It's been a pleasure to meet you,' he told Eva, and grinned at Sophie. 'Take care.'

'Now he's the kind of dazzlingly gorgeous man I thought only existed in my imagination,' the redhead declared, when Diether had driven off. She took Sophie's coat and hung it in the cloakroom. 'I adored his voice — it was like honey oozing over gravel.'

Sophie sighed. When her friend enthused, her enthusiasm sometimes went over the top.

'Believe me, he's far from perfect. I was thinking

that I'd like to visit Bonn again later in the year,' she went on, 'maybe in the autumn.'

'Come and stay with us,' Eva said, promptly and obligingly. 'Why not make it around October the third, which is now a national holiday? It commemorates the day of East Germany's reunification with West Germany,' she explained.

'Sounds perfect,' Sophie agreed, 'and thanks. Where're the girls?' she asked, for the quietness made it obvious that her former charges must be out.

'At their ballet classes. Giles is picking them up on his way home from work, so they should be here at any moment. Before they arrive, let me show you your room,' Eva said, shepherding her up the stairs, 'and your outfit for this evening.'

'Outfit?' she questioned.

'Everyone's expected to wear fancy dress and masks. I meant to tell you when I rang, but I forgot. Still, it doesn't matter because I know your size and—you've not gained or lost any weight?' She stopped to check.

'No.'

'Good—so I chose an outfit for you,' Eva completed. 'As you know, Giles and I have become heavily involved in amateur dramatics here,' she said, veering off at another tangent as she led the way into a small bedroom prettily decorated in blue and white. 'It's the amateur dramatics group we'll be with tonight. They're a friendly bunch. You'll like them. Anyhow, I was allowed a free run of a warehouse where theatrical costumes are stored. It was like an Aladdin's cave,' she said, her eyes shining. 'There were clothes which had been used in historical productions and pantomimes and——'

Sophie gave a groan. 'You've not arranged for me to go as the back end of a horse or something, have you?'

The redhead laughed. 'No. I shall be wearing a spangled crinoline and Giles is to be a duke in a scarlet velvet tail-coat and tights, but you're very demure.' She opened a wardrobe and took out a short white chiffon dress, trimmed with gold braid. 'You're a vestal virgin. This is your wig,' she said, showing her a mass of peroxide-blonde curls, 'and this is your mask.' Made of stiff white lace, the mask was cat-like and would cover the upper part of her face. 'Do you approve?'

'*Ja*,' Sophie said, then paused as she heard the sound of the front door being opened.

'Has Sophie arrived yet?' a child's voice yelled.

'Is she here?' called another.

'Has she come?' demanded a third.

Sophie looked at Eva and smiled. She was in the midst of friends and, for tonight, she could relax and—thank goodness—forget all about Diether.

Walking to the top of the stairs, she gazed down on three little girls. 'She has,' Sophie declared, and braced herself for the ensuing stampede.

CHAPTER FIVE

GILES sipped his *crème de menthe* and took a pull on his cigar. 'You don't look in the least like a vestal virgin to me,' he declared. 'You look like Marilyn Monroe. The hair's identical, and as for the dress——' He gave a low wolf-whistle.

Sophie tugged at the white chiffon which covered her breasts. Although the dress had seemed demure enough on the hanger, it plunged surprisingly low at the front and was backless to the waist, so she had been unable to wear a bra. Also the knot which secured the halter-neck at her nape had an unfortunate habit of loosening, which caused the chiffon to slide capriciously out of place.

'You don't think it's too revealing?' she asked.

Her former employer nodded approvingly.

They were sitting at a crowded dinner table, among many other crowded tables which were arranged at one end of a vast, garlanded ballroom. A tasty meal of melon, veal and a melt-in-the-mouth lemon dessert had been eaten, and now coffee and liqueurs were being served. The mood was mellow and expansive, and the room ran with the babble of conversation, interspersed with frequent peals of laughter.

'No, it isn't,' Eva protested, interrupting her chat with a chain-mailed Crusader to intrude. 'The dress may be a little more adventurous than you usually wear, but *Karneval*'s a time for being daring and, besides, what does it matter when no one knows who you are?'

Sophie grinned. 'I suppose it doesn't. After all, with you in your powdered wigs and masks, I can barely recognise you and Giles.'

'You don't recognise me from this?' the diplomat enquired, patting his paunch.

Her eyes danced. 'Well. . .now that you mention it your aptitude for good living is becoming something of a trademark.'

'You impudent little ——' he began, in mock anger, but stopped as a cheer rang around the room. The band had appeared and were taking their places on the stage. 'In punishment, you shall dance the first dance with me,' he declared.

As Eva had said, the amateur dramatics crowd were friendly and, after dancing with Giles, Sophie was partnered in rapid succession by the Crusader, a fugitive from the space age, and several other exotic characters.

'It's rather warm in here,' she said, as she completed an energetic whirl with Giles, who had claimed her for a second time, 'so, if you'll excuse me, I'll go and get a breath of fresh air.'

Walking out into the foyer, Sophie stood by the entrance for a minute or two where it was cooler, and then went to the rest-room. She washed her hands, adjusted her blonde curls, and, because the halter-neck had eased again, retied the knot. She inspected her reflection in the mirror. Although she had been paid sufficient compliments to know she was pretty, she had regarded herself as pretty in a healthy, outdoors sort of a way, but tonight, she acknowledged, she looked every inch the sultry glamour-puss.

Returning to the ballroom, Sophie paused in the doorway to survey the scene. The band was playing rock 'n' roll, and on the floor people twisted, shouted, they hippy-hippy shook. She smiled, infected by the gaiety, then her gaze wandered from the jigging masses and away to the bar, which was at the opposite end of the room to the dining area. Here a tall, lithe man was standing with one foot on the brass rail, sipping beer from a glass offered by a girl whose body gave off frank sexual invitation. The man wore a full-sleeved white silk shirt, tan suede waistcoat and matching trousers, and was, presumably, dressed as a yeoman. He had his back to her, but when he moved his head she saw his profile. During the evening several of the merry-makers had shed their masks, and the man and his partner had shed theirs. Sophie felt a thud of shock. Her heart jolted. The yeoman was Diether.

How. . .? Why. . .? Which perverse twist of fate had brought him here? she wondered in confusion. When he had spoken of socialising, she had assumed he would be entertaining the Italians again, but although he was with a group of people they were clearly his friends. So did this mean the girl was his girlfriend? No reference had been made to his having a woman in his life, but why not? He was an eligible and good-looking man, and no matter how distraught he had been it was five years since his wife had died. Sophie scrutinised the girl. With a bee-stung mouth, porcelain skin and long flaxen hair, she had the kind of face which graced magazine covers. And, clad in a cheeky hot-pant suit, pink

feather boa and pixie boots, the kind of figure which
drew gasps. Pity she spoiled it all by being the look-
at-me-don't-you-think-I'm-wonderful type, Sophie
thought, and then realised she was being catty.

All of a sudden, Diether pushed the glass away
and, standing back from his companion, turned to
scan the room. His gaze searched the dancers and
moved on until, reaching Sophie, it stopped. Dead.
As their eyes meshed, the breath caught in her
throat and her pulse began to race. They must be
over twenty yards apart and between them people
were dancing or noisily chattering, yet there was
something in his look which made her feel as if they
were together and all alone. Sensation rippled
through her. He seemed to be talking to her with his
eyes. Sharing a two-way hotline. Sending intimate
messages.

Sophie straightened her shoulders. Once again,
she was being foolish. Diether sent no message. He
was surprised to see her, that was all — and doubtless
none too pleased. She was deciding she would nod
and beat a hasty retreat to her table, when a glimmer
of a smile touched his mouth and he began to make
his way purposefully through the crowds towards
her. Her stomach contracted. For the first time since
her arrival in Germany she had been at ease, and
now he was coming to spoil it. Damn him.

'Dance with me,' Diether appealed, in German,
as he reached her.

Behind the cat mask, her brows rose. All she had
anticipated was a brief and sardonic enquiry, but the
evening's joviality seemed to be affecting him, too.
For a moment Sophie hesitated, jittery about the
prospect of partnering him, but a refusal seemed

churlish, so she said, '*Danke*,' and walked ahead of him on to the floor.

The rock 'n' roll session had ended, and, as they joined the clusters of couples, the lights dimmed and the band began to play the first notes of a love song. In anticipation of being held in the conventional manner, Sophie raised a hand, but Diether placed both arms around her waist — which left her no alternative than to rest her hands on his shoulders.

'I apologise for using the oldest chat-up line in the book,' he said, as they began to move in time to the music, 'but don't I know you?'

He had not recognised her! Sophie's eyes widened in surprise and she almost laughed out loud. But if he did not know who she was, then it must follow that he had been looking at her and had asked her to dance because he fancied her, she realised — and felt a spurt of smug feminine satisfaction. So what did she do now? Rip off her mask and declare, 'Fooled ya?' She could, but. . . Hadn't Diether proved his susceptibility to the 'eyes across a room' syndrome, and wasn't she now being given an opportunity to show him that, like his brother, he was not immune from being in thrall to desire? Her mouth twitched. Mischief bubbled. Should she give it a try — or, at least, make a few first inroads? Why not? Having him go weak-kneed over her would be an apt way of paying him back for his insults and hostility. Sophie hesitated. But when she spoke he might recognise her voice.

'I don't think so,' she said carefully, also speaking in German.

'Then we must've been lovers in a previous life.'

Her pulse tripped. 'Lovers?'

'How else do you explain the electricity?' Diether asked, smiling deep into her eyes. 'And don't deny that it affected you too.'

'I may have noticed a slight buzz,' Sophie agreed.

So far, so good. Her voice had not given her away, but, of course, he had never allowed her to speak to him in his own language, and the fact that she was so fluent would put him off the scent and deter him from making a connection.

'A buzz? I was struck by a hundred thousand volts, right here,' Diether declared, clasping his heart. 'If you don't believe me, feel,' he said, when she laughed, and he took hold of her hand.

As he pressed her fingers to his chest, Sophie felt the heat of his skin beneath the thin silk and the beat of his heart. Her own heart began to thud and she hastily took her hand away. He might be far from perfect, but there was no denying the potency of his charm when he chose to exert it. However, it was important that she be in control, which meant she must make the moves.

'I believe you,' she replied, and paused. 'But doesn't your girlfriend have the same effect?'

Diether cast a glance over to the bar, where his companion was pouting and looking aggrieved at having been deserted.

'Anna is not my girlfriend.'

'She'd like to be,' Sophie observed.

He shrugged. 'Perhaps.' He drew her closer. 'You're not here with anyone special either. I know because I've been watching you all evening.'

Below the cat mask, her mouth curved. 'Unable to take your eyes off me?'

'Hypnotised,' Diether declared.

Sophie laughed again, and wound her arms around his neck. She had never deliberately acted the vamp before, yet it was as though she knew the rules of the game by instinct. The disguise had made her abandon her normal caution and become reckless. And hadn't Eva said *Karneval* was a time for being daring, and wasn't today the day for the fairer sex to live it up? Though maybe her recklessness had something to do with the wine? she thought. She had drunk more than usual. Whichever, it was exciting to flirt and to be held close. The crowd on the dance-floor meant there was no room to do much more than sway, and as they moved she was deliciously aware of her soft curves pressed against the leanness of his body. Careful, warned a voice from a little corner of her mind, you're playing with fire.

'What's your name?' Diether enquired.

Sophie hesitated. What he had said and the way he was holding her were proof enough of his desire, so maybe she should end the pretence? After all, it would only need Eva to spot them and call a hello, and her cover would be blown. But when she glanced at the dinner table she saw that the redhead was deep in a discussion.

'Marilyn,' she told him.

His mouth tweaked. 'You stand over hot-air vents and let your dress whirl up around your waist?' he enquired.

'Twice daily.'

'I shall make certain I'm at the next performance.'

For a while, the teasing banter continued but gradually, as the love song was replaced by another and another, they fell silent. The mood between

them sobered and became tranquil. Diether slid his
hand up the silken length of her spine and, at the
gentle pressure of his fingers, she rested her head
against his shoulder. It seemed the natural thing to
do.

'It's weird, I can't remember where or when, but
I'm certain we've met before,' he said, drawing back
to study her as the dance came to an end. He smiled.
'Let's go and have a drink.'

Sophie nodded. 'Good idea.'

Now it seemed it only needed time, and the penny
would drop and Diether would realise who the girl
behind the mask really was; so in the bar she would,
she resolved, reveal her identity.

'Not there,' he said, when she turned towards the
groups of drinkers. He took hold of her hand, his
grasp warm and compelling. 'Upstairs.'

Because people were queuing and thinking that
somewhere on another level would be far less
crowded, Sophie went with him through the foyer
and into the elevator. He pressed a button for the
sixth floor and, when they emerged, took her into a
broad corridor which had bedrooms on either side.
Halfway along, Diether stopped at a door and took
a plastic keycard from his waistcoat pocket.

'You're—you're staying here?' Sophie enquired,
in confusion.

'*Ja*,' he replied, inserting the card into the lock.

As the door opened, he clasped her waist. In a
fluid movement, he drew her with him inside,
twisted her around, and steered her back against the
door. The room was dark. She could see nothing.
Disorientated, she raised a hand and found it spread-
eagled against his chest.

'I'm not in the habit of bringing strange women up to my room,' Diether murmured, his voice coming out of the blackness. 'But you don't seem strange, you seem. . .right,' he said huskily, and bending his head he kissed her.

The unexpected pressure of his mouth on hers destroyed any ability to think, to move, to protest. Taken by surprise, Sophie stood immobile, but as his tongue probed seductively a yearning spiralled inside her and her lips parted. With a low murmur of satisfaction, Diether began to kiss her eagerly and hungrily. She clutched at his waist. The taste of him, the moist seduction of his mouth, the scent of his skin in her nostrils were having a heady effect, and if she had not held on there was a danger she might have fallen.

'Ever since I first saw you, I've been longing to kiss you,' he whispered against her mouth, and he kissed her again.

This is madness, the voice protested from the corner of her mind, but Sophie did not listen. She wound her arms around his neck and strained closer. Diether had said she seemed 'right', and the sexual magnetism was mutual — and irresistible. Abandoning herself to the desire which he was igniting inside her, she responded to his kisses — until her skin felt hot and the tips of her breasts pulled and hardened.

'Let me take off your mask,' Diether murmured.

'No!' Sophie protested, in sudden alarm. Things between them had happened so fast and gone so far that now her identity could not be abruptly — shockingly — revealed. First she must prepare him, by explaining her motivation. 'I'd like to keep it on for a little while longer,' she said, feverishly wondering what on earth she was going to say.

Her eyes had grown accustomed to the dark and in the faint light of the moon which shone behind the curtains she saw him shrug and smile, reluctant but prepared to indulge her.

'As you wish,' he murmured, and reached for her again.

Sophie's head told her she must end the charade right *now*, but her body acted the traitor. There was a moment when she resisted him, but the touch of his mouth on hers worked its magic and her defences crumbled. No man had ever aroused her like this before, so quickly, so completely, she thought, half in delight, half in despair. Her arms were entwined around him again and her fingers were threading into the thickness of his blond hair, when, all of a sudden, she felt the halter-bow give at the nape of her neck. Sophie gasped and jerked back, but as she did the white chiffon slithered down to her waist.

In silence, Diether gazed at her naked breasts, the smooth skin silvered by the moonlight, the full, high curves mysterious and tempting in the shadows.

'Oh, God,' he muttered.

He raised his hands and tenderly caressed her breasts, then he began to circle his palms over the tight, rigid points of her nipples. Sophie shuddered, gritted her teeth, laid back her head. For a split second she submitted to the exquisite agony, but then she gave a strangled sob.

'Diether——'

He drew away. 'How do you know my name?' he enquired.

'Well——' she said, and stopped to take a controlling breath.

'You heard someone say it to me,' Diether decided, and bending his head he started to press a line of burning kisses from her shoulders down to the swell of her breasts.

'Please, no,' Sophie whimpered.

'Please, yes,' he said hoarsely. 'I want to lick you, to suck you, to taste you. I *need* to.'

At long last sanity reasserted itself and, summoning up all her will-power, all her strength, she placed her hands against his chest and pushed him violently away.

'And I need this to stop,' Sophie said.

'Why? I don't understand,' he protested, then broke off as the sudden peal of the telephone sliced like a clarion call through the room. The phone was beside the bed and he turned to scowl at it, then swung back to her. 'Why the sudden change of heart when——?'

She hauled up her dress. 'Answer it,' she said.

Diether seemed reluctant but, at a second ear-splitting peal, he strode over, switched on a bedside lamp and lifted the receiver.

'*Ja*?' he demanded.

Hastily Sophie retied the bow at the back of her neck. Thank goodness for the telephone! It had come to her rescue by allowing her to make an exit. Now the awkward and intensely embarrassing revelation of her identity could be avoided, for she would sneak out, make some excuse to Eva, and leave at speed in a taxi. Diether was half turned away and, as he waited for the switchboard to connect him with his caller, she reached for the handle and quietly opened the door.

'Helene?' he queried, and made a curt sound of impatience. 'This is not a good moment.'

Sophie stood stock-still. His stepmother was ringing? But why? What could have happened? There was a pause while he listened.

'It'll just be stomach ache,' he said irritably. 'Leave it for a couple of hours and see how the kid gets along, and if you're still worried I suppose you'd better ring me again.'

She frowned. Helene was calling about Rudy, so did she make her get-away while she could or should she risk staying to hear more? She was undecided and dithering when he spoke again.

'You're at the hospital in Bonn?' Diether said, in astonishment.

Sophie's heart sank. Her blood ran cold. Agitation formed a queasy layer in the pit of her stomach.

'And what's their diagnosis?' he enquired. During the lengthy silence which followed, she was on pins. 'OK, I'll be there as soon as I can,' he said at last, and jettisoned the phone. He swung round. 'I'm sorry, but I have to leave.'

'I'm coming to the hospital too,' she told him.

'You?' he protested.

Sophie removed the mask and peeled off her wig. 'Me,' she said.

Diether stared, then he uttered a furious and highly obscene expletive.

CHAPTER SIX

THE Mercedes swept out on to the road. At last the snow had stopped falling and the night was clear. High above in the sky shone a silver moon, its rays adding a sheen to the white which iced the world and reflecting a myriad diamond-glitters.

'What did you hope to achieve by deceiving me and trying to seduce me?' Diether demanded, in tight-lipped fury.

'I wasn't seducing you,' Sophie protested. She stared straight ahead through the windscreen. 'I was merely demonstrating that as Johannes and Lisette had been carried away so, given the appropriate stimuli, you were susceptible, too.'

'The appropriate stimuli being to bat your lashes, snuggle up to me, fall so spectacularly out of your dress?' he rasped.

'That was an accident! I don't want to talk about it now,' she went on hurriedly. 'I want to know what Helene said about Rudy.'

After revealing her identity, Sophie had gone straight down to the ballroom to speak to Eva, collected her coat, and joined up with Diether again in the foyer. Their walk out to the car had been swift and silent.

'That he'd woken up several times during the evening and been distressed,' he said, in clipped tones. 'In her wisdom, she decided to phone the doctor, but he was out on another call, so she rang for an ambulance and took Rudy to the hospital instead.'

'What do they say is wrong?'

'They don't. When she telephoned, she'd only just arrived and he had yet to be examined. And apparently he'd calmed down again—though that didn't stop Helene from insisting he could be at death's door. She asked if I'd go and provide some moral support, and she's obviously worked herself up, so——' He raised and lowered his shoulders.

Sophie cast him a glance. Diether might be hard-headed, but he was not hard-hearted. Far from it. Knowing their stepmother's propensity for flapping, many men would have promptly dismissed her appeal or said they'd speak to her in the morning, but he had responded—as no doubt he had responded to her appeals in the past.

'How exactly was Rudy distressed?' she enquired.

'He was drawing up his legs and screaming.'

'Had he been sick?' Sophie asked, wondering if Helene could have been plying him with an over-abundance of food again.

'She didn't mention it. He'll have—what do you call it?—colic, that's all.'

They had reverted to speaking English again though, given her current agitation, Sophie was relieved to do so.

'Rudy doesn't usually suffer from colic,' she protested, and frowned. 'How long will it take us to reach the hospital?'

Diether heaved an impatient sigh. 'You're not panicking too?'

'No. . .but I'd like to be there as soon as possible.'

'Yes, ma'am,' he said tersely.

The twenty minutes which followed showed Sophie just how fast a Mercedes sports car could go — which was faster than she had ever been driven before. At first, as the speedometer needle climbed steadily past the hundred mark, she viewed it with alarm, but it soon became clear that Diether was in full control. His hands were firm on the wheel. He anticipated corners and the actions of other vehicles. He knew what he was doing.

But *she* had not known what she had been doing when she had embarked on her charade earlier, Sophie thought bleakly. Neither had she been in control, nor anticipated. The idea that she was teaching Diether some kind of a lesson had been sheer self-pretence. She had wanted him to hold her close. She had revelled in his kisses. Remembering how she had wrapped herself around him and how aroused she had become, Sophie shifted uneasily in her seat. How could she have been so wanton and so abandoned? Her cheeks burned. She had humiliated herself, she acknowledged in sick realisation. Unstintingly.

When they reached the large modern hospital, enquiries at the reception desk revealed that Rudy had been taken to an infants' ward. Down what seemed like miles of silent corridors they trekked, until eventually they met up with Helene, who was sipping tea in a waiting-room.

'At last!' she exclaimed, dropping the cup down in the saucer with a clatter and leaping up. She looked at Sophie in bewilderment. 'How did you — ?'

'We were attending the same dinner,' Diether said briefly.

'Oh. Oh, well, I'm so glad you've come,' she gushed. 'Rudy's bound to feel happier if he knows you're here.'

'How is he?' Sophie enquired.

'The little mite suffered another attack about a quarter of an hour ago, but now he's been given something to calm him. The doctor's having a look and should be back with a report shortly. I realise you think I'm making a fuss over nothing, Diether,' she continued, 'but if you'd witnessed how Rudy—' Helene broke off as a clean-cut young man in a white coat strode through the door. 'How is he? What's the verdict? It isn't something— something life-threatening, is it?' she questioned, her voice shaking and her plump features awash with anxiety.

The doctor shook his head. 'No.'

'You're sure? You really—'

'I'm certain,' he told her, in a tone which said he found her agitation a trifle wearing. He swung to Diether and Sophie. 'Good evening. And you are?'

Helene hastened to introduce them. 'This is my stepson, Herr von Lössingen, and this is—' she hesitated, at a loss as how to describe her '—Sophie.'

The doctor shook their hands. 'From the symptoms he's displaying the baby appears to be suffering from an infolding of the small intestine, and this will require surgery. However, his condition doesn't seem to be too far advanced, so the telescoped piece should be easily put back into place.'

Helene seized Diether's arm. 'Rudy's to have an—an operation?' she faltered, the blood draining from her face.

'It isn't a major one,' Sophie said soothingly, although she, too, was shocked and dismayed. 'A baby which a friend of mine once looked after suffered from the same trouble and he was only in hospital for a few days.'

The doctor shone her a look of gratitude. 'Yes, there's no cause for alarm. We'll operate in the morning, so chances are Rudy'll be home by Wednesday or Thursday. And there should be no after-effects. I'm sure you and Herr von Lössingen must be anxious to see him,' he carried on, smiling at Sophie, 'so please come with me.' When Helene made as if to accompany them, he raised a hand. 'Why not sit down and finish your tea?' he said, the suggestion sounding more like a command, and she sank down again.

'I get the impression my stepmother's been something of a nuisance,' Diether said drily, as he and Sophie were ushered out.

The young man smiled. 'I'm afraid so. Twice earlier, the baby was drifting off to sleep until she insisted on picking him up and disturbing him. I understand you share the same house, so that's something you'll need to curb when he's convalescing. Her motives are good, but she's just a little *too* enthusiastic.' Pushing open swing doors, he took them into a darkened side-ward which contained six cribs, three on either side. In each, a tiny bundle lay sleeping. 'Here he is,' he said quietly.

Rudy was flat on his back, his arms stretched above his head. His eyes were closed, and his breathing was calm and regular. Sophie's throat tightened. Tears welled. Poor little boy, she thought. You started off fighting for life in Intensive Care, and here you are in hospital again. Crouching down beside him, she softly clasped her hand around his tiny one in the hope that, somehow, he would absorb her presence and feel comforted.

'He'll be OK,' Diether whispered, beside her.

She swallowed hard, then straightened. 'I know.'

'To have your child hospitalised, even for a few days, can be traumatic,' the doctor said, as they walked from the room, 'but we have accommodation here so, Frau von Lössingen, perhaps you would like to come and stay, and be close to Rudy?'

Frau von Lössingen? Sophie registered the title in surprise. The young man must believe she and Diether were married, and that Rudy was their son. Though it was an easy mistake to make, she reflected. They had arrived together and were of suitable ages. Expecting Diether to briskly disown such a connection, she waited for him to speak, but when he opened his mouth it was not to set the record straight, but to say he felt her moving into the hospital would be a good idea.

'What do you think?' he asked her. 'You were supposed to be going to Eva's, but——'

'That can be cancelled,' Sophie said quickly. 'I want to be with Rudy.'

The doctor nodded. 'As he's settled there's no need for you to stay tonight, so I suggest you return in the morning around nine. That'll allow you time with him before surgery.'

'I'll be here,' she promised.

He gave brief details of the accommodation and facilities which were provided for stay-in visitors then, as a nurse emerged from an office to speak to him, bade them farewell.

'I'll see you tomorrow, and don't worry,' the

young man said, with an encouraging smile, and disappeared.

In the waiting-room, Helene had finished her tea. 'How was Rudy?' she asked.

'Sleeping peacefully,' Diether assured her, 'and we've arranged that Sophie'll move into the hospital while he's here.'

'Move in? But where will you stay?' the older woman asked, and as they walked back through the corridors Sophie explained about the bed-sitting rooms which the doctor had described.

They were entering the reception area when a taxi drew up outside the glass doors and began to disgorge passengers. Seeing it, Helene hurried forward and waved a restraining hand at the driver.

'You two will be returning to your dinner dance, so I'll say goodbye.' She drew her coat around her. 'You see, I wasn't making an unnecessary fuss. I was following my instincts and they were right,' she told Diether, with *grande dame* haughtiness and, having delivered this parting shot, she climbed inside.

'I'm not going back to the hotel, I'm going to Eva's,' Sophie said, as the taxi drew away. After the débâcle in his room and now the prospect of Rudy undergoing an operation she had no taste for frivolity. She inspected her wristwatch. It was half-past midnight. 'She and Giles won't be home yet, but I have a key so I can let myself in.' To one side of the hall there was a telephone link for ordering taxis, and she gestured towards it. 'I'll fix myself a cab.'

'I'll drive you to Eva's,' Diether said.

She shook her head. 'It's out of your way, and your friends will be wondering where you are, and——'

'We need to talk.'

Sophie's stomach clenched. She knew exactly what the subject under discussion would be. Well, the recriminations would have to be faced sooner or later, and, she supposed, it might as well be sooner.

'All right,' she said, steeling herself, and, out of automatic good manners, added, 'thank you.'

In silence, they returned to the car and, in silence, Diether drove out of the hospital grounds and into the city streets.

'How far were you intending to go with your "demonstration"?' he demanded. 'As far as sleeping with me?'

'Of course not,' Sophie replied tightly.

'So your crusading zeal to make me believe Rudy sprang from Johannes's loins does have its limits?' he taunted.

'Yes! I stopped. . .everything, didn't I?'

Diether flung her a scurrilous sideways glance. 'But you know and I know that, given the appropriate stimuli, you wouldn't have needed much coaxing to continue.'

She flushed, thinking how the stimuli would have been his hands and his mouth moving tantalisingly over her body. But was he right? Would she have continued all the way through to the dizzying, glorious finale? Despite her talk of being so gripped by desire that caution was thrown to the winds, she had always imagined it was something that happened to other people, not to her. She had never visualised becoming so impassioned or so reckless — but she could no longer be sure.

Sophie turned to frown at his profile. 'There were two people involved in what happened this evening and, if you recall, you made the first move,' she said, moving from the defensive on to the attack. Her behaviour might have been ill-judged and imprudent, but he could not claim to have been the soul of discretion either. 'Were you intending to sleep with me?' she challenged.

Diether's laugh was heavy with scorn. 'You think I'm totally nuts?'

She did not think he was nuts at all; what she did think — now — was that she had asked a nutty question. She might have come perilously close to losing control, but him? Never.

'You approached a complete stranger and proceeded to — to woo her,' Sophie said, hastily launching an alternative broadside.

'But, as I've already told you, I thought I knew you.'

'You mean you thought we may have been introduced in the dim and distant past or you'd once spotted me waiting in a bus queue?' she enquired witheringly.

Diether scowled. 'I mean there was something about your face which reminded me. . .which made me feel. . .something which told me I wanted to. . .' He abandoned his struggle for a coherent explanation. 'You were mighty ready to come upstairs with me,' he accused.

'I was under the impression we were going to another bar,' Sophie informed him, with *froideur*. 'I didn't realise you meant us to have a drink in your room, because I had no idea you were staying at the hotel. Why are you staying?' she asked.

'Because I need to be at my office in the morning

in order to sign the Italian contract, and I decided that if it snowed all night it'd be wiser to be close.'

'Well, when we reached the bar — as I imagined,' she continued, 'I was going to come clean. Only the minute we reached your room you made a grab.'

Diether's fingers tightened around the steering-wheel. 'But all the time we were dancing you'd been draped over me.'

'So?'

'I was aroused. Maybe I wasn't thinking with my brains but with some other part of my anatomy,' he said, in an aggravated voice, 'yet if I was driven by lust so were you. Yes?' he insisted.

As his eyes met and held hers, sexual awareness throbbed in a silent beat between them. Sophie knew he was recalling how she had stood there in ecstasy while he had caressed her breasts, and so was she.

She wrenched her eyes away. 'Yes,' she muttered, for it seemed futile to try to deny it.

Though their circumstances were very different, she reflected. Diether's desire had been entirely physical, whereas hers had stemmed from having mentally absorbed — and unconsciously taken a liking to — plenty of other data about him. Sophie frowned. Although this could be said to give her a sounder motive, it was nevertheless regrettable. All her instincts rebelled against the idea of liking *him*, a man who considered her guilty of subterfuge and who treated her as though she were the carrier of some contagious disease. And, she realised, as if to add insult to injury, he had not lusted after her, Sophie Irving, but for some peroxided fantasy *femme fatale*!

'You prefer blondes?' she enquired coldly.

'Not necessarily.'

'But you have a weakness for the showgirl type?'

Diether's mouth thinned. 'No.'

'So you just act the Don Juan with whichever woman should happen to catch your eye?'

'What are these, multiple choice questions?' he rasped, and fell silent, apparently preferring not to risk any further gibes of a similar nature.

When the silence continued, Sophie heaved a sigh of relief. While she could not claim to have emerged from their combat triumphant, she did consider that she had managed to hang on to her dignity — albeit by her fingernails.

'I took out travel insurance, so paying for Rudy's medical care won't be a problem,' she said, her mind returning to the child they had left behind. 'I have the policy with me, but I'm not sure what I'm supposed to do.'

'If you give it to me, you don't need to do anything,' Diether told her. 'I'll sort out any financing with the hospital authorities tomorrow. I'll also explain that Rudy is not related to you. . .' he paused '. . .or, so far as we know, to me.'

Sophie cast him a look. Could she interpret that 'so far as we know' as a concession? He had agreed her story could be true, so was he now admitting that Rudy had a genuine claim to the von Lössingen name? No, it was wishful thinking. Diether wouldn't be swayed by mere words — *her* words — he would require cast-iron evidence, and doubtless lots of it.

'The hospital will be able to identify Rudy's blood-group,' she said. 'Do you know Johannes's?'

He shook his head. 'No.'

'But it could be on a medical record somewhere?'

'Possibly.'

'If you can find it, then we can see whether they match,' Sophie said. 'And they will.'

'But plenty of people have the same blood group, so it wouldn't prove anything,' Diether protested.

'Maybe, but it'd move Johannes and Rudy one step closer,' she asserted.

'You think so?' He sighed. 'I'll check with his doctor.'

Helene pushed aside the magazine she had been reading, inspected the lacquer on her fingernails, then retrieved the magazine and began to flick restlessly through it again.

'The operation's taking a long time,' she said, with an anxious glance at the clock. 'Do you think there might have been complications?'

Sophie winced, the question slicing deep into her, but her expression was calm when she turned from the window. 'No, I don't,' she replied. 'And the doctor said Rudy should be out of the theatre at *around*——' she emphasised the word '——eleven-fifteen, and it's only twenty past.'

'Maybe, but——'

'Any moment now someone will be ringing through, as promised, to tell us that Rudy is fine and to ask if we'd like to go and see him.'

'You're right,' the older woman said, comforted, and returned to her magazine.

Once again, Sophie gazed out at the snow-covered lawns which surrounded the hospital. If Helene made one more pessimistic reference to Rudy's current situation, she would *scream*. She, too, felt agitated, and having to pacify fears and provide repeated reassurances was a chore she could have well done without this morning. Still, at least his grandmother had arrived too late to see the baby before he was taken off to the theatre, she thought gratefully — too late to disturb him and unsettle him with her nervousness. Recalling the time they had spent together earlier, Sophie smiled. Although pale of face and subdued, Rudy had made his pleasure at being cradled in her arms blissfully apparent. She sneaked a look over her shoulder at the clock. She wished someone would report back — *now*.

When the phone rang a minute or two later, Sophie grabbed it up.

'Yes?' she demanded, and was advised by a nurse that, as anticipated, the operation had been straightforward and successful.

Weak with relief, she joyfully told Helene, and together they sped to the ward. Not content with the nurse's report, the older woman insisted on a face-to-face confirmation from the sister in charge that all was well, but finally she was convinced.

'So there's a happy ending,' she chirruped, smiling down at Rudy who was still groggy with the anaesthetic. 'Grandma has a luncheon to attend, so she must go now, *mein Schatz*, but she'll be here tomorrow to see how you're getting along.'

Sophie accompanied her to the entrance hall, but when Helene went off to find her car she returned to the ward. The sister had said that if she wished to remain with Rudy until he recovered from his drowsiness she could, and so she sat beside the cot watching as, with blinks and snuffles, he gradually came awake.

'He seems happy enough,' remarked a nurse who had come to check on him.

'He does,' Sophie agreed thankfully, 'but would you mind if I stay with him a little longer?'

The nurse grinned. 'Go ahead.'

For a while she spoke to him, softly assuring him that he would soon feel better, and the baby gazed at her with knowing blue eyes. But eventually his lids grew heavy and he fell asleep. Sophie studied him. Helene had shown her photographs of Johannes when he was just a few months old, as a schoolboy, in his twenties, and she, too, believed she could see the similarity between Rudy and his father. Would he look like him when he grew up? she wondered. She grimaced. Although with shaggy blond hair, a beard and a moustache Johannes von Lössingen had been handsome, it was in a cavalier, devil-may-care kind of a way. Yet, if his hair had been cut and his jaw shaved, perhaps he would have looked stronger and more solid? More like Diether. She gazed at the baby. It was strange to think that Diether—so tall and commanding—had once been this tiny, this defenceless.

Sophie sighed. She seemed to be forever thinking about Diether. Despite worrying over Rudy, hardly ten minutes had gone by today without some runaway image of him or some remembered remark he had made sneaking into her mind. And last night she had lain awake for hours reliving what had happened between them at the hotel.

'How did the operation go?' a familiarly deep voice enquired and, startled, Sophie looked up to find the subject of her thoughts standing beside her.

She jumped to her feet. 'It went perfectly. Rudy's

on course to make a full recovery,' she told him, and then, to her great astonishment, she started to cry.

When Helene had been around she had needed to take charge and be brave, but now all her bottled-up anxiety broke free. Her shoulders shook, her breath came in shudders, the tears streamed down her face.

'I'm — I'm being silly,' Sophie gasped.

Diether smiled and put his arms around her. 'No, you're not,' he said.

The tenderness in his smile and in his embrace made her sob afresh. If he had told her to pull herself together, she could have managed it — just — but his compassion jerked a nerve deep inside her. For a long time the tears fell, but eventually Sophie sniffed and blew her nose.

'I thought you'd still be busy with the Italians,' she said.

He shook his head. 'I got rid of them at the first opportunity and came straight over. I reckoned that, between having to cope with Helene and agonising about the baby, you could be finding life a bit trying.'

Sophie nodded. 'I was, and thank you.'

In the days which followed, Diether continued to visit the hospital. Rudy rapidly regained his health and so Sophie's peace of mind was restored, yet every evening he called in on his way home from work. At first this surprised her, but then she realised that when his stepmother raised doubts about the baby's progress — and, despite all the evidence, she would be bound to do so — his daily visits meant he could dispel them.

On Tuesday, the doctor decreed that Rudy had

recovered enough to be released the following morning. When Helene arrived, she passed on the good news and the older woman said she would inform Diether. That evening when he failed to appear at his usual time Sophie concluded that, as the baby would be home tomorrow, he had decided not to bother. She did not blame him. He had a heavy workload and it made sense.

She gave the baby his bottle, settled him down for the night and went back to her room. The hospital boasted a coffee-shop which served excellent food, but it was too early for dinner and so she decided to read for a while. Sophie was stretched out on the sofa, when someone knocked at her door. Thinking it would be a girl who was in residence to be near her toddler and with whom she had struck up an acquaintance, she called a cheery, 'Come in,' but it was Diether who entered.

'You haven't decided to give tonight a miss,' she said, in surprise.

'No. I was delayed at work.'

Swinging her feet to the floor, Sophie stood up. This was the first time he had been to her room, and she felt suddenly conscious of their being alone together in what was, primarily, a bedroom. There might be a sofa, television and a drop-leaf table, but the majority of the space was filled by a candlewick-covered bed. And now, yet again, her mind flew back to the time they had been in his hotel room. . .

'Do you want to go and see Rudy?' she enquired, gesturing towards the door.

Diether shook his head. 'I've already looked in on him, and he seemed fine.'

'Then why are you here?'

He unbuttoned his leather coat and pushed his hands into the pockets. 'I've come to ask if you'd be willing to stay on and look after Rudy.'

'I would. I am,' Sophie said immediately. The prospect of leaving Helene to care for the baby while he was convalescing had been troubling her, and she had decided that, if it was suggested, she would remain. 'I'll stay until he's had his stitches out, which should be in a week or so.'

'No, I meant will you stay on as his nanny? I know you said you weren't interested, but that was when ——' he hesitated '— things between us had got a bit over-heated. However, now I'm offering you the job.'

'So I'm not such a hazard after all?' she enquired defiantly. 'You've decided that if I've worked for a diplomat I can't have a criminal record, and you're prepared to risk having me around? Thanks for the vote of confidence.'

Diether frowned. 'Look, I ——'

'No, I won't stay on as Rudy's nanny,' she said, cutting him off.

'I'll pay you excellent money.'

'I don't want your money and I don't want the job,' Sophie said firmly, and a little fiercely.

'But you caring for him is the ideal solution,' Diether protested. 'Rudy would be happy, you get on well with Helene, and Axel thinks you're ——'

'I'm not caring for any more children,' she insisted. She tilted her head. 'Helene hasn't mentioned the idea of employing a nanny to me, so I presume you haven't mentioned it to her?'

'Not yet. I don't seem to have had the chance to get around to it. You're sure you won't consider the idea?' he enquired, shining the kind of smile that would have had birds flocking out of trees.

'Positive. Eva mentioned a friend of hers who'd hired an excellent girl through an agency in Cologne,' Sophie went on, 'so I could ask her for the number and fix up for them to send some people out to the house.'

Diether considered her suggestion. 'OK. You know the right qualities to look for and the right questions to ask, so would you be willing to take part in the interviews?'

'Yes,' she agreed, thinking that although it was something of an about-face for him to want *her* opinion she would welcome the opportunity to have an input into who cared for Rudy.

'But before anyone's offered the position I want to see them,' he added. He cast her a look. 'Will you stay until a nanny's been installed?' he appealed.

Sophie sighed. The extra week she had envisaged in Germany seemed to be stretching into two, or even three.

'All right,' she said.

Diether smiled. 'Thank you.'

When he had gone, she sank back down on the sofa. He had reckoned that her looking after Rudy would be the ideal solution, Sophie brooded, but it was not. For if she cared for the baby she would be living in the same house as *him*. She would see Diether every day, talk to him every day, and this, her instincts warned, would inevitably lead to her caring more about him — caring a lot — and there could be nothing ideal about that!

CHAPTER SEVEN

AFTER stating the intention to look after the baby single-handed, Sophie wondered whether Helene might regard the employment of a nanny as a personal affront and raise objections. On the contrary. She declared herself fully in favour — though it was always possible she could be bowing to Diether's wishes. Whether or not, the agency was duly contacted, and in the days which followed they sent round a number of applicants, one of whom met all the criteria. So on Saturday afternoon the girl attended for a second interview, and this time Diether was present.

'Well, what do you think?' Helene enquired, hurrying back into the drawing-room after she had shown the girl out.

Her stepson rose and lazily stretched, his sweatshirt riding up to reveal a strip of smooth brown skin above his jeans.

'Too young,' he decreed.

'She's the same age as I was when I started,' Sophie told him.

'And too talkative.'

'You asked for her views on childcare and she gave them,' she protested.

'But it took her a full ten minutes.'

'She's enthusiastic, which is good.'

'Maybe she was a bit gossipy,' Helene reflected, frowning out at the girl as she disappeared on to the street, 'and having someone like that constantly around could become a little wearing.'

Sophie suppressed the urge to shriek. She considered the nanny was satisfactory in every way and so had his stepmother, until Diether had criticised.

'Do you want the agency to send along another batch next week?' she asked him, reining in her irritation.

'Please.' He turned towards the door. 'I'm going to wash the cars.'

'And my charity ladies will soon be arriving for our committee meeting,' Helene said, as he went outside. Moving around the room, she became busy, plumping up cushions, straightening ornaments, readjusting blooms in the flower vases. 'While they're here, you're very welcome to use the study,' she told Sophie.

'Thanks, I will,' she said. 'There're a couple of letters I'd like to write, so I'll do them now while Rudy's asleep.'

Not much later, Sophie installed herself in the quiet book-lined room on the opposite side of the hall. Although she had telephoned her parents to let them know that her stay in Germany was being extended, she wanted to give a fuller explanation. And she needed to drop a line to the neighbour who was keeping an eye on her house. As she wrote, the repeated ring of the doorbell and the sound of voices indicated that the committee members were assembling.

Sophie had finished both letters and was licking the envelopes, when she felt a sudden sense of being under observation. She stiffened, a chill shivering down her spine, then turned to find Axel lolling against the door-frame watching her. How long had he been there? she wondered. On several occasions since her return from the hospital she had noticed him silently gazing. At first she had decided he must be willing her to realise that he was an irrefutably dishy young man, but now it seemed more a case of infatuation. This was how the pursuit the previous year had begun, she thought, in alarm — with her being spied upon, mutely monitored, beadily eyed. But the circumstances are different, common sense insisted. Axel is a youth smitten by calf love, that's all, and you are not under threat. Yet when he walked forward emotion proved stronger than logic, and Sophie's heart began to race and goose-bumps prickled her flesh.

'I think you're lovely,' he said.

She managed a polite smile. 'Thank you.' Gathering up her letters, she got to her feet. His closeness was making her feel claustrophobic. 'See you later,' she said and hurried out past him out into the hall.

Axel followed.

'Why don't we take Rudy for a walk?' he suggested.

'He's asleep.'

'Then how about us having a walk together? The snow's gone and it's a sunny day, so we could go to the park.'

Sophie shook her head. 'No, thank you.'

'Would you like to watch a football match?' Axel persisted. 'My college team is —'

'Sorry, I'm busy,' she said, wishing he would stop hassling her and desperate to get away.

'Why? What are you going to do?' he asked.

Sophie was frantically searching her mind for an

answer which would act as a foolproof and final deterrent, when Diether strode out of the kitchen. He had completed his car-cleaning and was rolling down his sleeves.

'She's coming for a drive with me,' he said.

Axel frowned. 'You and Sophie are going out together?' he protested, in a voice which veered between disbelief and petulance.

Diether curved a proprietorial arm around her waist and drew her against him.

'We are.'

The youth looked sulky. 'In that case, I shall watch the football on my own,' he declared and, grabbing his jacket from the hall-stand, he stomped out of the house.

'Thank you for coming to the rescue,' Sophie said, stepping back.

His embrace might be purely a piece of play-acting, but it was unsettling none the less. Dressed casually in the navy sweatshirt and with his legs encased in tight denims, Diether seemed raunchily and overwhelmingly masculine—and her hormones were on red alert.

'I overheard the conversation and thought you sounded to be becoming a bit uptight,' he explained, 'but I meant it about us going out.'

'You want to take me for a drive? What for?' she asked, immediately suspicious.

Hooking his thumbs into his hip pockets, he stood with legs apart. 'To show you the Rhine. Although you've been here for a fortnight you haven't had a chance to do any sightseeing, and it'd be a crime if you returned home without taking a look.'

Torn, Sophie hesitated. A run along the world-renowned river valley did appeal and yet, firstly, she felt unsure about being with Diether in the confined closeness of the car, and, secondly, she was wary of his reason. She had, she recalled, been misled by his seeming kindness before, and why should he want to spend the afternoon escorting *her*?

'What about Rudy?' she asked.

'When he wakes up, Helene can deal with him. Even with a nanny, she's going to have to look after him on the girl's days off,' he said. 'Besides, she'd like nothing better than a chance to show the baby off to her friends. You get your coat, and I'll tell her she's on stand-by duty.'

'I appreciate the sacrifice you're making,' Sophie said, still prevaricating, 'but——'

'Do you think I have an ulterior motive?' Diether demanded impatiently. 'As a matter of fact, you're right. I'm not making any progress with my enquiries and I want to have a chat. Now, go and get ready.'

What he intended to do, he explained as they motored down through Bad Godesberg, was cross to the opposite side of the Rhine and drive south, then, after thirty or forty miles, cut back over the river and return via the left bank. This meant that their journey would start by them taking a ferry and it was not long before the Mercedes was nosing in among a dozen or so other vehicles for the five-minute sail. As the ferry began to move slowly across the water, they left the car and stood in the wintry sunshine.

'We land at Königswinter,' Diether said, pointing ahead to the opposite bank, where a row of pollarded trees grew in front of pretty pastel-shaded houses. 'It's a popular holiday town and in summer is crowded with visitors. However, if you walk up into the Drachenfels——' he indicated forested crags which formed a green backdrop '—there are plenty of quiet paths.'

'Nice,' Sophie muttered, barely listening.

His declaration that he wanted to chat had filled her with resentment—she had *known* he could not be taking her up the Rhine out of the goodness of his heart—but also with foreboding. Aware that as soon as his enquiries produced something positive he would tell her, she had refrained from requesting a report. Maybe it could be classed as cowardice, yet she had preferred not to rock the boat. But did his lack of progress mean he was now about to tell her that she must take Rudy and go? Sophie wondered, her head throbbing. It would explain his veto of the nanny—whom, whatever he had said, he must have recognised as being entirely suitable.

'See the ruin on the top?' Diether went on. 'That's Drachenfels castle.'

Some show of interest seemed to be required, so she shaded her eyes against the sun and squinted at the distant tower.

'*Drachen* means dragon,' Sophie stated.

He nodded. 'According to the tales of the Rhine, a dragon once lived on the hill and it was slain by Siegfried who then bathed in its blood to make himself invincible.' A brow arched. 'Mind you, every hill, or island, or rock around here seems to come equipped with its own legend.'

When the ferry docked, they drove through the quaint little town and turned south. With its green slopes, vineyards, and a string of castles perched on high, the river valley more than lived up to its reputation for scenic beauty. Yet as Diether continued to point out places and regale her with the history of the locality Sophie became increasingly distracted.

'You said your enquiries weren't progressing,' she reminded him, unable to stand the agony any longer.

'No. Johannes's medical records have gone missing so there's no record of his blood-group,' he explained, 'and the bank manager's unable to trace a cheque or a bank draft made out to Lisette for any amount, let alone five thousand pounds.'

Despair made her lungs feel tight and congested. While the blood-group idea had always been second string, she had been certain the bank could, would, *must* provide confirmation of her story.

'Lisette definitely received the money,' Sophie protested. 'When she told me about it, I could see from her face how amazed and touched she'd been.'

Diether moved his shoulders. 'There's no knowledge of any kind of transaction, so——'

'So you consider the whole thing is a figment of my imagination?' she demanded.

A moment ago she had been despairing, but her despair was rapidly converting itself into anger. Anger because the fates seemed cruelly determined to thwart Rudy's cause. Anger because Diether retained his infuriating—and now seemingly justifiable—doubts about her. Anger because, yet again, she had been unfairly placed in the wrong and thrust on to the defensive.

'I didn't say that,' he replied.

'You didn't need to,' Sophie retorted.

'Look——'

'Or maybe you think it's Lisette's imagination which has gone haywire?'

'Well——'

'Johannes sent her that money!' she declared, marching the words out in jackboots.

'Sophie——'

'If it was a question of imagination why pick on five thousand pounds?' she rampaged on. 'If Lisette had wanted to make her story sound more believable, why didn't she plump for five *hundred*? Or, on the other hand, if she was being entirely fanciful why not make it *fifty* thousand? But she didn't, she——'

'Could I have a word?' Diether demanded, annoyance raising his voice and tightening his mouth.

Sophie glowered at his profile. 'Go ahead.'

'*Danke*. If you'd let me finish, I was going to say that Johannes had a tendency to be secretive and so I've asked if enquiries can be made to discover if he could have had an account with another bank which, for some reason, didn't come to light when he died.'

'I see,' she mumbled, her anger breaking down.

'However, as yet nothing's materialised and it seems unlikely. So I thought that if you could tell me more of what Lisette said about their relationship it might spark off an idea for a fresh line of enquiry,' he completed.

Relief washed over her. Diether did not intend to give Rudy his marching orders—yet. And he never would, if she could possibly prevent it.

Now Sophie tugged at her lip, trying to recall the brief, fragmented, often on-the-run conversations from the past. Lisette had had a confusing habit of gossiping about people without naming them and throwing in facts willy-nilly; and even when she had realised the girl was referring to her German boy-friend she had not paid too much attention. After all, it had not seemed important *then*.

'Well, within days of their meeting he was telling her he loved her, and vice versa. To me, Lisette seemed to be searching for stability and, for a while, she thought she'd found it in him. Though he didn't strike me as too wise a choice.'

'Why not?'

Sophie frowned. Her last remark had been tacked on without thinking, but what could she say now which would not be too provocative, too slanderous? Although she might regard Johannes von Lössingen as a parasite and a layabout, he was Diether's brother.

'He sounded to be the kind of individual who — ' she chose her words with care ' — had a happy-go-lucky approach to life.'

'What you mean is that he was a spoilt boy with a singular distaste for anything approaching sweated labour,' Diether said pithily.

Sophie gave him a startled look. 'Er — yes.'

'You're right — though there were reasons.' He hesitated. 'I guess I'd better explain.'

'Please.'

For a minute or two Diether frowned at the road ahead, gathering his thoughts. 'To start at the beginning, I need to tell you about my father and his attitude towards Helene,' he said. 'Dad was twenty-five years her senior and, whereas he and my mother had been equals in age and equals in their marriage, he treated her like a pretty child who needed to be protected and indulged. And as she's full of insecurities she lapped it up.'

'What was your mother like?' Sophie enquired.

'Independent, strong-minded, resourceful. If something had to be done, she didn't dither and ask for everyone else's advice first, she just did it.'

'And her genes were passed down to you,' she said.

Diether cast her a droll sideways glance. 'Is that a compliment?' he enquired.

'It's an observation,' Sophie replied coolly. 'Helene told me you were seven when your mother died,' she continued.

'That's right, and nine when my father remarried.'

'How did you get along with Helene?' she asked.

'Very well. She fussed, but she was loving, and loving was what I needed. Both my parents had been averagely firm with me—when I needed a telling-off, I got it,' Diether continued, 'but if my father reprimanded her boys Helene became upset and so they were allowed to do more or less what they wanted. When they were small this didn't matter too much, but as Johannes reached his teens his behaviour grew increasingly wilful. He refused to comply with the most reasonable request, he was always answering back, and he started to play truant from school. I was away at college so I didn't see him too often—thank God, because he became downright objectionable.'

Sophie remembered how he had once described her. 'A royal pain in the butt?' she said archly.

His gaze was steady. 'Precisely.'

'Was this about the time your father became ill?' she enquired.

He nodded. 'Johannes needed someone who could be firm and knock him into shape, but Dad didn't seem able to summon up either the energy or the will. Instead he abrogated all responsibility to Helene, who denied that her son was fast becoming a hooligan. She continually made excuses and, because Johannes could wrap her around his little finger, was always giving him money. Excessive amounts.' Diether frowned out at the hills which were bathed in pale gold sunshine. 'Because he was this tearaway kid with a seemingly endless source of cash, all the dead-beats and free-loaders for miles around gravitated towards him—with the result that he became the ringleader of an extremely dodgy group, who drank heavily and caused trouble wherever they went. Eventually there were so many complaints that Helene was forced to admit Johannes was woefully out of control. She appealed to my father for help and he went through the motions of acting the stern parent, though in reality he was beyond caring—but it didn't make a blind bit of difference. Then he died, at which point Helene switched her requests for assistance to me.'

'What did you do?' Sophie asked, when he sighed.

'I tried to get Johannes to behave by appealing to his better nature, but I was wasting my time. The tragic part was——' Diether cast her a look. 'You said something about Lisette needing stability—well, I always felt Johannes craved that, too. Deep down, he seemed to want to be *made* to conform, to be part of the steady, worthwhile mainstream of society, but he'd been allowed to run amok for so long that he fought like hell against it.'

'And, of course, you fought back—like hell,' she said crisply.

'Why is it I get the impression you regard me as something akin to Attila the Hun?' he asked.

Sophie arched a brow. 'I wonder. How did you fight back?'

'I told Helene to quit financing him and informed Johannes that if he wanted cash he must earn it.'

'Which presumably did not go down well?'

Diether's laugh was dry. 'If I hadn't been bigger than him I'd have been the victim of grievous bodily harm!'

'Yet you gave him a job at Von Lössingen's,' Sophie remarked.

'It was not my choice, but he lacked the qualifications to find employment elsewhere and, as Helene insisted *ad nauseum*, he was my father's son and Dad had founded the firm, and——' He rapped his fingers on the steering-wheel. 'Anyway, stopping the hand-outs and forcing him to spend time at the office did help, in that the doubtful friends made an exit and he cut down on his drinking. This didn't happen overnight, indeed it took years, but in the twelve months before he died Johannes did appear to be quietening down. Mind you, the contribution he made to Von Lössingen's was minimal. I did my best to keep him chained to his desk, but it was a constant battle—and I had a company to run.'

'Lisette said he always had time to take her out for lunch, or to the races,' she recalled.

'Yes, with the best will in the world Johannes was pretty feeble in the work-ethic department. He was going to Australia ostensibly to search out fresh business, but I knew darn well he'd spend most of his time lying on the beach.' Diether's mouth tilted downwards. 'Not that he'd ever have admitted it, nor anything else he got up to. As I mentioned earlier, he was secretive. He refused to live at home and rented a down-at-heel apartment, but Helene and I were never allowed to know what went on there.'

. 'The way you didn't know about Lisette.'

He nodded. 'Or about Johannes going to the races — as far as I was aware he'd never been to a racecourse in his life.'

'Or about the five thousand pounds. You say the bank can't produce evidence,' Sophie began earnestly, 'but maybe they could check again, because I can assure you that —'

Diether cast her a diminishing glance. 'Is this "provoke a man" week?' he demanded.

'Excuse me?'

'You're obviously gearing up to bark at me again, but don't bother, because I've had enough,' he said.

'But Diether —'

'*Finito!*'

She glared at him, then sighed. As desperate as she was for her account to be believed, to be verified, reiterating everything would be about as productive as banging her head against a brick wall.

'That looks an interesting place,' Sophie remarked, as a picturesque village of half-timbered houses and stone towers appeared in the distance.

'Suppose we stop there?' Diether suggested. 'We can take a look around and have a cup of coffee.'

'Thanks, I'd like that,' she agreed.

After parking the car, they strolled up through an ancient arched gateway into a maze of narrow cobbled streets. On either side were painted wooden houses which, at first glance, looked medieval but had, so their plaques revealed, been painstakingly reconstructed. Many were adorned with friezes of proverbs or blessings, and as they wandered around they paused to translate them. The bustling market-place was explored and a splendidly Gothic town hall, then Diether took her through an alleyway of wine cellars and inns to a cosy restaurant.

'Axel told me the two of you had had some battles,' Sophie remarked, when a waiter had brought mugs of rich dark coffee. 'Presumably that was when you were in the process of knocking *him* into shape?'

Diether thrust her a suspicious frown, but then, deciding she was not in the business of condemning him, nodded.

'Axel's the reason why I moved back in with Helene,' he said. 'You see, although he was never anywhere near as unruly as Johannes, a couple of years ago he fell in with a crowd she didn't feel happy about. They seemed to be having a bad influence, and Axel became boisterous and started coming home drunk; and when he did Helene found it difficult to cope. She was terrified he might end up like Johannes and asked if I would move in, so that I'd be around to give assistance if required.'

'Don't you mean to take command?' Sophie asked, with an impish grin.

He shrugged good-naturedly. 'I guess. Naturally Axel resented it when I arrived and started to wield the big stick, but he's a good kid at heart and eventually he saw sense.' Diether looked at her across the rim of his mug. 'I realise that having him drooling over you must be a bit of a nuisance, but he means no harm. Axel's popular with the girls, even if he is the first to say so, and now he's fancying his chances with——' he gave a faint smile '—an older woman, that's all.'

'I know. It's just that he makes me feel. . .nervous. I was dismissed from my last job,' Sophie said, deciding that, as Diether had been frank about his brothers, she would be frank, too, 'and that happened because the wife believed I was chasing her husband. Naturally I wasn't——'

'Why naturally?' he cut in. 'As I recall, you did a pretty efficient job of chasing me at the *Karneval* dance.'

She felt the heat seep into her cheeks. 'I did *not* chase you!' she protested. 'As I've already explained, all I ever intended——'

'Calm down,' Diether protested. 'It was a joke. I know you're not the kind of girl who'd make a play for a married man.'

'Oh. . .thanks,' Sophie muttered, and took a restorative sip of coffee, gaining time and self-possession in the movement. 'The trouble with the husband began by him worshipping me from afar, like Axel,' she said. 'The whole experience was so unsavoury that it's made me paranoid about being stared at, and now I'm permanently on my guard. Too much so.'

'Do you want to tell me about it?' Diether said.

Sophie hesitated. She had never thought that when they had set off in the car they would spend the afternoon swapping confidences, but should she explain what had happened? Why not? Although an outline had been sketched for her family and friends, she had never gone into detail—and now the opportunity to talk to him seemed surprisingly attractive.

'Yes,' she said, then frowned, not knowing how to start.

'What age was the guy?' he prompted.

'Late forties. Roger was an old father, and his wife, Glynis, was in her early forties, so she was a geriatric mother.'

'What children did they have?'

'A little girl of three, and a year-old baby. The kids were great,' Sophie said, with an affectionate smile, 'and, initially, I got on well with Roger and Glynis. They both worked in television and lived in one of the smart neighbourhoods of London. They seemed to be so happily married,' she continued, getting into her stride. 'They were always kissing and cuddling, and saying how much they loved each other. I would've sworn Roger was the original doting husband, which is why I failed to pick up the warning signs.'

'Which were?' Diether queried.

'When I looked back afterwards it was clear that Roger had been ogling me over a period of months and, whenever he could, making attempts to touch me.' She shuddered with distaste. 'When he first started to gaze, naturally I noticed it, but I decided he couldn't actually be *seeing* me and that he must be daydreaming. And if he passed me and brushed against me, or if he handed me something and our hands touched, again I didn't think anything of it.' Sophie paused. 'Or mostly I didn't. There were times when it seemed as though he might be doing it on purpose, but I told myself it must be my imagination. I mean, this was a man who never let a day pass by without vowing utter devotion to his wife. This was a pair who were considered to be the ideal couple by all their friends, a pair who did seem to be genuine love-birds.'

'Marriages are not always what they appear,' Diether said gravely.

'This one wasn't! Anyway, one evening when Glynis was working late, Roger appeared as I was making myself a drink in the kitchen and announced, I quote, that he had "the hots" for me.'

'And?' he enquired, when she frowned over the memory.

'I thought it must be some kind of joke, until he lunged and started trying to kiss me. I pushed him away and speedily explained that the feeling was *not* reciprocated, but he lunged again. So I fled up to my room with the intention of locking myself in, but he came after me. My room was on the third floor and Roger was a good twenty pounds overweight, but, boy, did he gallop up those stairs!' Sophie said wryly. 'Before I had a chance to lock the door, he barged in and stood there, purple in the face and panting, telling me in graphic detail what he intended to do to me. I was scared stiff. I tried to reason with him, but he forced me down on to the bed. At which point Glynis walked in. She'd arrived back earlier than expected, heard voices and decided to investigate.'

Diether grimaced. 'Oh, lord!'

'It was a relief to be rescued, but——' She blew out a breath. 'Before I could speak, Roger leapt to his feet and started to tell her how I'd asked him into my room on the pretext of changing a light bulb. He said that the minute he'd appeared I'd confessed to having a mad crush on him, put my arms around him and manoeuvred him down on to the bed. I insisted he was twisting everything around and that he'd chased me, but she refused to listen.'

'And you were told to leave?'

Sophie nodded. 'Glynis ordered me out of the house immediately. It was so degrading, so embarrassing, so unfair. And when I went back the next day to pick up my things Roger was there leering at me when she wasn't looking.'

Diether reached across the table and fleetingly touched her hand. 'A sordid little man and a sordid incident,' he said sympathetically.

'I'd already found leaving the children I'd cared for hard to handle,' she went on, 'but what happened with Roger finally convinced me that I didn't want to be a nanny any more.'

'And not wanting to be a nanny is why you won't stay on and care for Rudy?'

She looked at him and looked away. 'Yes,' she said, thinking that it was partly true.

'So what do you intend to do?' Diether enquired.

'Something where I can use my German. I passed it at A level and during my three years with Eva it was our lingua franca,' Sophie explained, 'and recently I've been brushing it up by attending conversation classes.' She finished her coffee and saw that his mug was empty. 'Shall we go?'

On their return to the car, they continued along the side of the Rhine for a few miles until they reached a bridge. Here they crossed over and headed north. They were on the final homeward stretch, when Diether indicated an ivy covered stone archway high up on a hill.

'That's the remains of Rolandsbogen,' he said. 'It was a castle which took its name from Roland, who was the nephew of the Emperor Charlemagne and his most famous paladin.'

'There's a legend attached?' Sophie enquired.

He grinned. 'Naturally. Roland, so the story goes, was betrothed to Hildegard. However, Roland went off to fight and the rumour came back from the distant battlefield that he had been killed. Hearing this, Hildegard was inconsolable, and she went to the convent of Nonnenwerth, which was on an island in the Rhine, where she took the veil and made eternal vows of chastity. But the rumour proved to be untrue and Roland returned, only to discover that his beloved was locked away beyond his reach. Now the only consolation left to him in his distress was to build a castle overlooking the convent, where he could gaze down and think about Hildegard, and where he remained until he died.'

'Ah,' she said, with a sigh.

Diether smiled. 'A story which tugs at the heartstrings.'

She nodded. 'Still, it's nice to know that true love and loyalty can exist.'

'Isn't it,' he said.

Hearing a sudden tautness in his voice, Sophie turned and saw that his humour had dropped away. He looked grim, yet somehow. . .vulnerable, and she did not need second sight to know he must be thinking about his wife and their relationship. Should she ask him about Christa? she wondered. No. This afternoon the mood between them might have been surprisingly open, but a remoteness in his gaze confirmed what Axel had said—that his marriage was not an area where enquiries would be welcome.

'Lisette talked about how she and Johannes spent a lot of time exchanging life histories,' Sophie said, taking a gymnastic leap back to his request for information. 'They also found they had a similar taste for junk food, and——'

The remainder of the journey to Bad Godesberg was spent with her determinedly dredging up snippets, though nothing she remembered seemed to have any significance.

'And that's about it,' she was saying, as they pulled back into the drive.

Switching off the engine, Diether turned to her.

'If Axel thinks you and I have something going between us he'll soon lose interest, so why don't we let him believe that?' he said.

Taken aback by the sudden and unexpected suggestion, she frowned. 'But——'

'You don't want him to continue making eyes at you, do you?'

'No-o,' Sophie admitted.

'Then that's settled,' Diether said decisively, and climbed from the car.

CHAPTER EIGHT

SOPHIE drew up the side of the cot and rested her elbows on rail. She sighed. One way or another, it had been a trying day.

In the morning, Rudy had had his stitches removed. The doctor had assured her that the procedure would be virtually painless, yet beforehand her nerves had been stretched as tight as piano wire and afterwards, when the baby had happily gurgled, she had felt limp with exhaustion. However, by the afternoon Sophie had found herself wanting to gurgle too. A procession of nannies had continued to beat a path to the door but they had been disappointing, until now when a second suitable candidate had appeared. Eager to settle the matter, she had conferred with Helene who had declared herself equally enamoured and it had been arranged for the girl to return a couple of hours later to meet Diether.

'You saw her, so you know she was a pleasant, friendly person,' Sophie said, speaking to Rudy, 'but he rejected her on the grounds that she looked as though she might be moody!' She sighed again. 'Still, at least this time your *grossmutter* didn't agree with him, so I suppose that's some kind of progress.'

The baby stuck his fingers in his mouth and noisily sucked them.

Smiling, she pulled up his quilt and bade him goodnight. Helene had gone to a friend's house to

play bridge, and when Sophie went downstairs she
joined Diether and Axel, who were watching television. Diether was sitting in the corner of the sofa,
one foot resting on a denimed knee, as she entered
he patted the cushion beside him.

'Sit with me,' he said.

Sophie hesitated. The suggestion that Axel should
be made to think they 'had something going' meant
that, over the past few days, Diether's attitude
towards her had taken an alarming veer towards the
physical. From time to time, he had held her hand,
stroked her hair, hugged her. All this had been done
in a free and easy way, and he was supremely casual,
yet each incident had registered high on her personal
agitation scale, been logged in her mind and repeatedly thought about afterwards. And now coping with
his brother's silent gazing was beginning to seem
infinitely preferable.

She gave a small smile and indicated an armchair.
'I'll sit here, thanks.'

'What's the matter?' Diether asked, reaching out
to catch hold of her wrist as she walked past. 'Are
you still mad at me because I didn't given the nanny
the all-clear?'

Trapped, Sophie frowned down. She had thought
she had disguised her irritation, but apparently not.

'As a matter of fact, I am,' she said, silently
chafing against the grip of the strong brown fingers
which handcuffed her arm. 'She had everything
going for her and, frankly, your claim that she could
be a manic depressive was a load of——'

'Drivel?' he supplied helpfully when she paused.

'Yes.'

'I disagree.'

'Well, you're wrong,' Sophie declared.

Diether pulled on her wrist, drawing her down so that she had no option but to bend over him.

'Like hell,' he said, grinning.

'You are!'

'Convince me,' he murmured.

'I beg your pardon?'

His grip tightened, and he gave a sudden tug which took her by surprise. Yanked off balance, Sophie grabbed out with her free hand to try and keep herself from collapsing, but he tugged again.

'Oh!' she gasped, finding herself inelegantly sprawled on top of him.

'If you were to kiss me,' Diether said, encircling his arms around her, 'there's a chance — just a slight one — that I could be convinced the nanny was worthy of consideration, after all.'

Kiss him? Sophie recognised this as yet another performance for Axel's benefit, and knew she should reply with some light-hearted, jokey put-down. Yet as she looked into the lean face which was just inches from hers her heart began to slam against her ribs. With thick fair eyebrows, a long straight nose and well-defined mouth, his features seemed like an endlessly fascinating landscape. She wanted to run her fingers over his face, and, yes, she wanted to kiss him. She wanted to feel the warmth of his lips on hers and push her tongue into his mouth, and —— As the realisation of what she was thinking hit, hot colour suffused her cheeks.

'Let me go!' Sophie protested and, now desperate to break his hold, she fought for release.

'If you wriggle around like that, there's an even

bigger chance of you convincing me,' he said, an unholy gleam in his eyes.

At his words, she became abruptly aware of the growing hardness of him against her thigh. Sophie's blood coursed through her veins. A tide of heat swept over her. It became difficult to breathe. That she might have such an effect on him had not occurred to her, though why not? Diether might be fooling around — and intent on fooling his brother — but he was a virile and healthy male. Very virile. Very male. And didn't she have past experience of the alarming ease with which flagrant sexuality could flare up between them?

'Let me go,' she repeated, and this time there was a plea in her voice.

'Sophie,' he responded, a sombre line grooving itself between his brows. 'I——'

'Would you two shut up?' a voice demanded crossly, and, abruptly reminded of the youth in the background, they both turned to see Axel staring at the screen. 'I'd like to hear what's being said on this programme.'

Diether clasped her waist, swinging her off him and around.

'Sorry,' he said.

'It won't happen again,' Sophie told the young man.

Diether's dark blue eyes met hers. 'No?' he queried.

She determinedly held his gaze. 'Never,' she declared.

Much to her relief, Diether recognised the request inherent in her statement and, in the days which followed, there was no more horseplay, no further seemingly affectionate caresses. Whether this was due to his simply deciding to comply with her wishes, or because he was reluctant to risk her arousing him again, or because he felt Axel had been sufficiently deterred, she did not know—but he kept his distance. Yet over the weekend Sophie reached the decision that she must leave Germany as soon as possible. All physical contact might have ended, yet it only needed Diether to walk into the house and she became overwhelmingly *aware* of him. A jelly of neuroses. On the brink of falling apart. It was a demeaning state of affairs, especially considering that, while no longer openly hostile, he continued to harbour reservations about her. It was also a potentially explosive state of affairs. The sexual chemistry meant that should Diether decide to make another advance she could be in danger of falling straight into his arms, and maybe even into his bed. And so it was a state of affairs which must be terminated.

On Monday evening, Sophie was waiting in the drawing-room when he returned from work. Helene had taken Rudy upstairs to give him his bath and Axel was studying, so she was alone.

'Today Helene and I saw another girl who we both think is the model nanny,' she said, after they had exchanged greetings.

Diether strolled to stand in front of the fire, his hands in his trouser pockets and his long legs set apart. 'So when am I going to see her?'

'You're not. At least, not until she reports for work next Monday. Helene's already spoken to the agency and hired her.'

'Without my approval?' he protested.

Sophie looped her hair behind her ears. 'Someone else was interested in her and if we hadn't finalised things today we could have missed her.'

'Suppose I don't like the girl?' Diether demanded.

'There isn't anything not to like,' she said briskly. 'Katrin is thirty. She's gentle but capable, and——'

His jaw hardened. 'I still want to see her.'

'Why—so you can find fault?' Sophie enquired. 'You asked me to sit in on the interviews because you said I knew which qualities to look for, and I *do*. Yet whenever I select someone—someone who Helene also considers is satisfactory—you refuse to trust my judgement.'

'It's not a question of that,' Diether said, frowning down at his feet.

'It is! It's just the same as you not trusting my judgement when I say Lisette is telling the truth about Rudy. It's the same as you not thinking I'm telling the truth and not trusting *me*. I know Helene always looks to you for guidance, but she's the one who'll be dealing with the nanny on an all-day, everyday basis,' she carried on, 'so isn't she the person who should make the final choice?'

'I'd still appreciate a look at the girl,' he said grittily.

'Suppose you take a look and you veto her; what happens then?' Sophie demanded. 'Another week is spent going through all the rigmarole of interviewing and at the end of it you turn your thumbs down yet again? I may have agreed to stay until a nanny was installed, but I never agreed to stay on indefinitely— and that's what it's beginning to seem like!'

Diether's brow furrowed. 'But choosing someone

who'll be living as a member of your household is
not something to rush into,' he protested.

'So see Katrin and give her the elbow if that's
what you want,' she said, losing patience. 'However,
don't expect me to be here to sift through the next
batch of hopefuls.'

There was a prolonged pause. 'All right,' he said
reluctantly, 'the girl is employed.'

She smiled. 'Katrin really is very nice.'

'And you'll remain for another week after she
arrives, to make sure she knows what she's doing?'
Diether enquired.

'I think two days will be long enough.'

'Only two?' He sounded put out and strangely
annoyed. 'You'll be leaving in—what, ten days'
time?'

'I will,' Sophie said firmly.

'I'm off now,' Helene declared, appearing in the
doorway of the drawing-room a few evenings later.

Sophie looked up and smiled. 'I hope you manage
to raise lots of money.'

'Thanks. Axel's due to join me at the hall at nine
o'clock, so if he isn't on his way by eight-thirty will
you remind him?' she asked, turning to Diether who
was finishing a cup of after-dinner coffee. 'He's lying
on his bed listening to music, and you know how,
when he does that, he has a habit of forgetting the
time.'

'Don't worry,' he said. 'I'll make sure he turns up
for duty, as required.'

When his stepmother had gone, Diether put his
cup and saucer aside on a low table.

'I've been doing a lot of thinking lately,' he said,

sitting forward with his hands gravely clasped between his knees.

'About what?' Sophie asked.

'You. . .and Rudy.'

Rudy? A flash-flood of panic swept over her. Sophie knew his investigations had not advanced and that their chat had failed to spark off any fresh line of enquiry, so could this be the crunch? Was she to cancel the nanny, remove the baby and take him back to England? She had fought her hardest and got nowhere, so maybe now she should grovel. Maybe she should kneel at Diether's feet and plead.

'What about him?' she asked tremulously.

'I agree that he's Johannes's son.'

Her brown-green eyes opened wide. 'You—you do?' she faltered.

'Yes, and if I'd had any sense I would've realised it long ago.'

'So he can live here and be brought up as a von Lössingen?' she enquired.

Diether nodded. 'Of course.'

Joy lifted her out of her chair and on to the sofa beside him. 'Oh, Diether, thank you,' she said, and, putting her arms around his broad shoulders, hugged him.

'You don't need to stop,' he murmured, when she abruptly broke away and sat back.

But there was every need. The hug might have been spontaneous and done without thinking, yet — even through her delight — Sophie had been aware that when they touched it was as though terminals were linking and a current was flowing through them.

'I—I—er——' What could she say? 'Thank you,' she repeated.

'You shouldn't thank me,' Diether said. 'You should bawl me out for being such a——'

'Dim-wit?' Sophie suggested, when he broke off to search for a word.

Although their conversation now travelled between English and German, mostly it was in English—as it was tonight.

He gave a wry laugh. 'And bone-head. And addle-brain. It's obvious that you're honest and, even though it may not have seemed like it, I think that, deep down, I pretty quickly ruled you out as a trickster, yet I clung on to the idea that Lisette might've tricked you. But the other day, when you accused me of a lack of trust, it made me stop and think. I *do* trust you.'

'Yes?'

'I swear on oath that I consider you to be a knock-out human being with the moral fibre of a multitude of saints.'

Sophie gave him an old-fashioned look. 'You're overdoing it,' she warned.

Diether grinned. 'No, I'm not. It's what I believe. *And* I trust your judgement, so——'

'Then how come you turned down the first two nannies?' she intruded.

Diether frowned and flicked a dismissive hand. 'That's a different issue; what we're talking about here is Rudy. So,' he continued, 'I began to ask myself why, when I respect your intelligence, I refused to admit you were right when you insisted Lisette's story was genuine. It didn't make sense, and in any case, as you said, why should she lie? She had nothing to gain from lying to you.'

'So you're won over?' Sophie said.

'In total. I know this is an excuse, but when we first met ——' He pressed his lips together. 'Well, for a number of reasons being suddenly confronted with a baby threw me. I reacted badly and, having started off that way, everything seemed to gather its own momentum and I found it difficult to change track. I've said a lot of things which I had absolutely no right to say, and I'm sorry.' He gave an appealing smile. 'Will you accept my apology for being so disbelieving, so damn sceptical?'

She nodded. 'Your apology is accepted.'

'Thank you,' Diether said soberly, and, raising her hand to his lips, he kissed her fingers.

When, instead of releasing her hand, he continued to hold it to his mouth, Sophie's heart started to pound. His indigo-blue eyes seemed to cast a spell, trapping her, and all she could do was gaze at him. *This is like the time at the dance,* she thought dazedly. *Diether looked at me across the room and——*

'I wish my mother wouldn't volunteer my services for these charity efforts of hers,' a voice complained, and Axel ambled in through the door. When he saw them together, he stopped and scowled. 'Sorry if I'm disturbing you.'

The spell shattered and Sophie hastily took her hand away. 'You're not,' she said, shining him a bright smile. 'How're the funds being raised this evening?' she went on, being determinedly conversational. 'And what're you going to do?'

'Videos are being shown of horse races and everyone bets on them, and a percentage goes to the benefit of deprived wildebeest or some such thing,' he explained gruffly. 'And my job is to go round all the old fogies and collect up their betting slips.'

Diether arched a sardonic brow. 'Smiling nicely and making polite small talk all the while.'

Axel grunted, and looked at his watch. 'I must go.'

'Have fun,' Diether instructed.

The young man's eyes skidded from him to Sophie and back again. 'And you,' he muttered sourly.

As the front door slammed shut, Sophie's brow puckered. The conversation had opened up an intriguing train of thought.

'If Johannes went to the races with Lisette, chances are he would've gone on other occasions, too,' she said.

Diether nodded. 'I imagine so.'

'And presumably when he went he gambled — so he could've won a lot of money.'

'Five thousand pounds?' he protested, instantly recognising what was on her mind. 'It would've needed to be a substantial wager to win so much, and I doubt Johannes would've had sufficient ready cash.'

'But he could've done?' Sophie persisted.

Diether pursed his lips. 'I suppose there's a possibility — a slim one.'

'Is there anyone you know of who might have gone racing with Johannes?' she asked. 'Someone who could say whether or not he ever had a big win?'

He thought for a moment. 'Hans-Joachim may be able to help. He's the son of one of Helene's friends, and he and Johannes used to knock around together,' he explained. 'Hajo's the black sheep of his family too.'

'Do you have his phone number?'

'Helene will have made a note of it in the address book.' He cast her a look. 'You want me to ring now and see if he's in?'

Sophie bobbed her head. 'Please.'

She went with him into the hall, where Diether found the number and dialled.

'Hajo?' he said.

Although only one side of the conversation was available to her, in the next few minutes Sophie heard enough to know that her spur-of-the-moment idea was, indeed, fact.

'Johannes did have a big win!' she exclaimed delightedly, as he replaced the receiver.

'The equivalent of seven thousand pounds,' Diether reported, and tilted his head. 'Isn't this the point at which you throw your arms around me and hug me again?' he enquired.

Sophie gulped in a breath. She did not know how he had managed it, but he had correctly defined what she had instinctively been going to do—until she had stopped herself.

'Hug you real close?' she said, adopting a flippant tone.

'So that our hearts beat as one.'

She pretended to consider the notion, then shook her head. 'No,' she declared decisively.

Diether shrugged. 'Worth a try. Hajo was also able to throw light on how Lisette received the cash,' he continued.

'He was?' Sophie said, in pleased surprise.

He nodded and gestured towards the drawing-room. 'Let's go and sit down, and I'll tell you all about it. Hajo wants to avoid trouble with his folks—which is why he's never mentioned this before,' he explained, when they were facing each other along the sofa, 'but apparently he and Johannes used to sneak off to the races on a fairly regular basis. Hajo restricted himself to bets he could afford, but Johannes had bigger ideas, and when a horse came along which he felt certain would win he'd borrow money from a pet money-lender and place a substantial bet. Unfortunately, the certainties didn't always gallop in first and he got into debt——' Diether grimaced '—and so, when he finally hit the jackpot, he decided it would be wiser to keep quiet. However, the win enabled him to settle all his debts, keep a tidy sum himself, *and* give Hajo, who happened to be visiting London the same week, five thousand pounds in cash to pass on to Lisette.'

'In cash?' Sophie said. 'So that's why there was no trace of any transaction at the bank.'

'*Ja*. Apparently Johannes received his winnings from the bookmaker in German notes and immediately changed part of it into English ones. And when Hajo asked if he wasn't being over-generous he said no, because it was a gift for his future bride who was carrying his child.'

'How did Johannes feel about the baby?' she enquired.

'He was over the moon.' Diether hesitated. 'And I'm also——'

Hearing a sound from upstairs, Sophie frowned. 'Rudy's having a moan,' she interrupted. 'I wouldn't be surprised if he's started teething. Tomorrow I'll get something to soothe his gums but for now, if you'll excuse me, I'd better go and see to him.'

His shoulders moved reluctantly. 'Carry on,' he said.

The baby grizzled for the next couple of hours and, although his disturbances came intermittently, they were sufficient to prevent any more serious conversation. However, around the time of Helene and Axel's return he settled, and when everyone went up to bed he was fast asleep.

As Sophie climbed between the sheets, she reached for her paperback. At long last, she was nearing the end and so she would read for a while, she decided—read and bask in the happiness of Diether's acknowledging Rudy as his nephew. She smiled. Everything she had wanted for the little boy had come true. He was with his family, and—— She listened. On the other side of the house, Rudy had whimpered again. For a minute or two she waited, but now there was silence. Sophie had started to read when she heard another distant whimper. She sighed. Should she go to him? But the whimpers were half-hearted and, besides, surely Helene would hear? She had returned to her book when, not much later, the baby gave a strident yell. Now Helene *must* have been alerted, but apparently, like Axel, she slept log fashion for, off and on over the next few minutes, his cries continued. Climbing out of bed, Sophie found her robe and pulled it on, though by the time she emerged on to the landing Rudy's cries had ceased. She set off determinedly towards his room, but as she drew near her step faltered and slowed. Diether was talking to the baby in a low, comforting voice, and then he started to sing.

Tiptoeing forward, Sophie peeped round the door. The room was lit by a small lamp, and in the muted glow she saw him holding the baby. All he wore was a pair of navy pjyama trousers and so Rudy, in a white towelling sleepsuit, was cradled against his bare chest. The sight of the man and the baby together brought a lump to her throat. Diether looked so muscular, so masculine, yet so gentle. And Rudy, who was gazing solemnly up at him, had nestled in his arms with an ease which seemed to say that this was where he belonged.

'*Schlaf ein, mein Prinzchen, schlaf ein,*' Diether sang, crooning a lullaby which she remembered Eva singing to her children. Sleep, my little prince, sleep, Sophie automatically translated.

As the lullaby came to an end, he raised his eyes and saw her. He smiled.

'You know,' he said quietly. 'I think Rudy looks like Johannes, too.' He laid the baby down and carefully tucked the covers around him. 'Now you're to close your eyes and go to sleep, and you're not to make another sound until the morning,' he said. 'Understood?'

'Yessir,' Sophie whispered, when Rudy's eyelids dutifully fell.

For a moment or two, Diether gazed gravely down on the child and then he joined her at the door.

'No one else appeared to have heard him, so I thought I'd see what I could do,' he explained, as they walked back along the landing.

'And you worked wonders,' she remarked, with a smile. They reached her door. 'Goodnight,' Sophie said.

As she turned to go, Diether lifted a hand and

gently ran his fingers up along the line of her jaw to thread them into the chestnut thickness of her hair.

'Goodnight, *Liebling*,' he murmured, and his eyes fell to her mouth and she knew he was going to kiss her.

Sophie took a backwards step. She was well aware that when she had hugged him so impulsively earlier Diether, too, had felt the current — but she had not wanted him to respond to it, either then or now. His kiss would be dangerous, seductive, and woefully addictive.

'I thought we'd dropped the charade that we're. . .involved?' she said, agitation adding a prickle to her tone. 'Axel isn't here, so there's no need for you to bother — though even if he were it isn't necessary,' she added.

Diether's brow furrowed. 'Say again?'

'Axel may still have a tendency to gaze, but it doesn't worry me any more,' Sophie told him, and stopped. She had started off by making a determined excuse to intercept him, but all of a sudden she realised that what she was saying was the truth. 'Telling you about the incident with Roger seems to have been therapeutic,' Sophie continued. 'Before being stared at upset me, but now I can handle it — so you can end the pretence.'

He looked at her through the shadows. 'It isn't a pretence,' he said, 'and it never was.'

'No?' Her eyes were wide and uncomprehending. 'But——'

'I may have reckoned it was for Axel's benefit and initially I told myself that, too, but when I touched you it was because I wanted to touch you, because I *needed* to.' Diether frowned as a creak of springs

from a room across the landing indicated that his
brother was turning over in bed. 'Let's talk in your
room,' he said, and before Sophie could protest he
ushered her inside and closed the door. 'All I needed
to do was tell Axel to stop gawping and he would've
done,' he went on, 'but I wanted an excuse to be near
to you. When Rudy woke up earlier this evening I
was about to say that as Johannes was over the moon
about Lisette being pregnant, so am I — because if she
hadn't been then you and I would never have met.
And,' he added huskily, 'I'm very glad that we did.'

Sophie took an unsteady breath. 'Oh,' she said.

She knew the response was inane, but, with her
head filling with bemused delight, it was all she could
think of.

'When we were at the costume ball I may not have
known your name,' Diether carried on, 'but subcon-
sciously I knew it was you.'

'How? What do you mean?'

'I recognised your mouth. Your tantalising,
delicious, tempting mouth,' he murmured, lifting a
hand to trace the outline of her lips with his finger.
'I didn't realise it at the time; all I knew when I
looked at you was a compelling attraction, but that
was why. You remember when we were outside
Eva's and a snowflake landed on your lips? I wanted
to lick it off. I wanted to kiss you. I wanted to tear
off your clothes and make love to you, right then
and there,' Diether said, his voice thick with feeling.
'And when I saw you at the hotel I immediately felt
the same. OK, it was instinctive, and it made no
sense on a logical level, but somehow I knew you
were a woman I was crazy about. And I am.'

'Y-yes?' Sophie stammered.

'Yes.' He gave a twisted smile. 'It's a good thing the Italian deal was finalised when it was, because now I seem to spend most of my time at the office lost in a daze, thinking about you,' he said, and he drew her into his arms.

At the first sensitive, exploratory touch of his tongue against her mouth, Sophie's lips parted. She wound her arms around his neck and pushed her hand into the fair hair at his nape, feeling its texture and its thickness beneath her fingers. As everything she had wanted for the baby had happened, so her own secret yearnings could be fulfilled, she thought ecstatically—for now she knew that the explosive awareness had been a two-way thing. And now the differences between her and Diether had disappeared, which meant there was nothing to stop them from falling in love, nothing to keep them apart.

He loosened her sash and slipped his hands inside her robe, sliding them slowly up over her ribcage to the swelling fullness of her breasts. As he drew his fingertips across the tight peaks of her nipples, Sophie's senses swam. Restlessly, she moved against him. She wanted to be naked. She wanted the fragile barrier of silk to be removed. She wanted to feel the heat and urgency of his touch on her bare skin—but she also wanted to touch him.

The glow from the bedside lamp glinted on the hair on his chest, turning it to spun gold. She lifted her hands and slowly stroked them over him, glorying in the roll of his muscles beneath his skin, in the rasp of hair.

'*Liebling*,' Diether murmured, the endearment a lingering verbal caress. His hands curved around her, travelling slowly down the length of her spine until they reached her buttocks. 'All it takes is for you to be close to me for three seconds, and the sensation is one of hardening of the organs,' he whispered, pressing her into his undoubted maleness.

Sophie smiled into his eyes. 'I've noticed,' she said.

Diether laughed softly. He kissed her again, and, as if by compulsion, his hands began to explore her body.

'You wouldn't care to fall out of your dress again?' he murmured, also growing impatient of the silken layer.

'If you insist,' she said.

'I do.'

Sophie stepped back and shrugged away the robe, then slowly unhooked the shoe-string straps from her shoulders. As the nightdress slithered down past her waist, across the slenderness of her hips and to the floor, Diether gazed at her with narrowed eyes. His look feasted on the high, swollen globes with their spreading wine-red aureoles, then roamed down over her abdomen to the secret bush of dark curls at her groin.

'I want you more than I've ever wanted any other woman in my life,' he muttered hoarsely.

'And I want you,' she said, then decided she must tell him the true extent of her feelings. 'Diether, I —' she began, then broke off, her head snapping round to gaze at the door in horror. Someone had knocked. 'Who is it?' Sophie enquired, hastily dipping down to the floor to slip her arms through the straps and draw her nightdress back on again.

'Me, Axel. I heard noises, so I know you're still awake.'

'If he comes in here,' Diether threatened, in a vicious undertone, 'I'll——'

'What do you want?' she called.

'To warn you about Diether,' the young man whispered fiercely. 'I know he seems keen on you, but don't be deceived into thinking he's interested in a long-term relationship. He isn't, and you know why? Because he's still hung up on Christa.'

'The bastard!' Diether said, an intensely ragged edge in his voice.

Sophie looked at him and, for a moment, their gaze met, but then he looked away. An icy hand clutched at her heart. His eyes—bleak and troubled—had been eloquent, and so was the nerve which beat in his temple.

'He's never been serious about anyone since Christa died,' Axel continued, 'and he isn't serious about you. All he wants is a roll in the—— *Verdammt!*' he exclaimed, as the door was suddenly wrenched open and he found himself confronted.

'What the hell do you think you're doing?' Diether demanded furiously.

The youth gulped and clutched nervously at his pyjama jacket. 'I—I didn't know you were here.'

'Obviously not,' he grated. 'And when I need you to make a judgement on my personal and private affairs I'll ask—but until then I'd be obliged if you did *not* interfere!'

'OK, OK,' Axel mumbled.

'I'd also consider it a great favour—and so would she—if you would quit ogling Sophie,' he snapped.

'I'm sorry,' the young man said, and, with a shamefaced smile, hastily backed away across the landing and into his own room.

The silence hung tense and laden between them.

'I must go,' Diether said. He rubbed savagely at his brow. 'I can't. . .we can't. . .not now.'

Sophie opened the door wide. 'Goodnight,' she said, in a stiff tone of finality.

He looked at her for a moment. 'Goodnight,' he replied, and strode away.

She tossed and turned until the early hours. She should have known that Diether remained in thrall to his wife, she thought despairingly. She ought to have realised he had no wish, no need for a replacement. Hadn't she seen his expression when she had remarked on Roland and Hildegard's true love and loyalty? Didn't she know that he still found it painful to talk about Christa? Diether might have said he wanted her more than any other woman in his life, yet he had not said he *cared* more, she remembered. Sophie's insides hollowed. The difference was significant. All he had ever had in mind with her was a physical fling, while she had believed they were at the start of a dedicated relationship—but sex without commitment was not her style.

She had come disastrously close to making love to him, she brooded. She had also been a word or two away from telling him she loved him—and making a fool of herself. A prize one. Sophie totted up the days until she was due to leave. There were five. Five days when she would, she resolved, do her best to keep out of his way and make sure she was never alone with him. Restlessly, she punched at her pillow. Then, next week when those five torturous days were over and she had placed hundreds of miles between them, she would begin the healing process.

CHAPTER NINE

'IT's so warm, it feels more like high summer than spring,' Helene remarked, peeling off the crimson serape which covered her woollen suit. 'You've chosen the perfect day for a walk on the Drachenfels.'

Sophie took a firmer grip on the baby-buggy. 'Yes,' she said.

'And I'm sure Katrin is going to be perfect as Rudy's nanny,' the older woman enthused.

'So am I. You don't. . .mind her taking charge?' she enquired tentatively.

'Frankly, it's a big relief.' Helene looked shame-faced. 'Thinking I could easily adapt to caring for a child at my time of life was rather optimistic.'

'Maybe,' Sophie agreed. She gazed down at the slipway where the first vehicles were being directed on to the ferry. 'I'd better board. Thank you for the lift.'

'You're sure you wouldn't like me to pick you up on your return?' came the query. 'I could arrange to be here at around——'

'Thanks, but it's no trouble for me to take a taxi.'

Helene opened her car door. 'Then enjoy yourself,' she instructed gaily, as she climbed inside.

Sophie gave a strained smile. 'I'll try.'

Enjoyment was an impossibility, she brooded half an hour later as she pushed Rudy up a woodland path. The sun might shine, the sky might be a cloudless blue, the earth beneath the trees might be carpeted in wild flowers, but her heart was heavy. Tomorrow she said goodbye to the baby. Tomorrow she returned to England. A bond had formed between Rudy and his grandmother, and already he seemed to be happy with Katrin—so he should not miss her too much. But she would miss him. The tears stung at the back of her eyes. Painfully. When Lisette had vanished, she ought to have kept quiet and kept him, Sophie thought, in a moment of anguished rebellion. No, she shouldn't. Even if it had been allowed, keeping him would have been selfish and not to Rudy's benefit. His present and his future were far brighter here. He had Helene to dote on him, a nanny to attend to the more mundane practicalities, Diether to provide material security and a steadying masculine influence.

Diether. Sophie swallowed. She was not going to cry over the baby, and she refused to cry over him. Over what might have been, if. . . The day after their aborted lovemaking—when dark smudges beneath his eyes had indicated that he, too, had spent the night sleepless and thinking—she had wondered whether he might tell her that his craving for the long-dead Christa had finally been reconciled and that *she* now held first place in his affections. Her hopes had been in vain. Diether was sombre, introspective, silent—and, recognising that his thoughts remained centred on his wife, her determination to avoid him had strengthened.

'*Guten Tag*,' a middle-aged couple in trilbies and hiking boots said cheerfully, marching past her on their way down the hill.

Sophie smiled and nodded a greeting. She had

planned to come to Bonn in the autumn, she reflected, as she walked on, but perhaps that plan should be scrapped? Seeing Rudy, content and established, would be a great comfort, yet how would she feel when she met Diether? Raw? Wounded? Wrecked? In the past she had had her fair share of boyfriends — including a long-term and serious one — but she had never felt as strongly about any other man as she felt about him. Her stride lengthened, her pace quickened. Diether might continue to grieve for his dead wife, but she would not be wasting endless and pointless amounts of time grieving over him — even if he was destined to be the love of her life.

'When I see Diether again, *if* I see him, I shall have recovered,' Sophie told the baby defiantly.

He grinned.

As they reached a leafy glade, the path split into two. Did she follow the gentle slope upwards, walking in the wake of a chattering foursome who were heading for the castle ruins, or should she go right on to a quieter track? Sophie wondered. Quietness won. Being in the vicinity of others did not appeal; her purpose in coming here today was to spend time alone with Rudy. Time bidding him a silent farewell. Time consoling herself that, no matter if there was a sick, dull ache in her chest, her decision to bring the baby to Germany had been the right one. For several minutes, she plodded on through the trees, but all of a sudden the forest ended and they emerged into brilliant sunshine. Sophie blinked. Ahead, on the side of the hill, a flat grassy area had been designated as a scenic viewpoint, and she wheeled the pushchair towards it. Sitting down on a rough-hewn bench, she shed her jacket and put on her sunglasses.

'See the river?' she asked the baby, pointing to where, far below, the Rhine curved like a wide blue snake. 'It's over eight hundred miles long and flows through three countries.' She indicated the barges, which looked as small as toy ships, sailing on the water. 'And see the boats?'

He grinned again.

Sophie gazed out at the springtime panorama. Lush forested slopes rolled serenely down to the river. Sunlight glinted on church spires in a sprinkling of distant villages. On the horizon, hazily glimpsed fields made a patchwork of green and yellow. She could understand why Diether liked living here, she thought, then frowned. She would not dwell on him again. What mattered now was the future, not the past. And her future would be busy.

Pushing up the sleeves of her white cotton sweater and determinedly planting her hands on her denimed knees, Sophie started to formulate a plan of action. On her return home, immediate steps would be taken to find herself a job. She would also put her grandfather's house on the market — the decorating was virtually complete — and buy a flat with the proceeds. Plus, she would end the somewhat boring friendship with the uninspiring young man. She had decided she would initially seek a position as an interpreter and had moved on to speculating how much the house was likely to bring, when Rudy gave a sudden chuckle. The pushchair was slanted out of the direct glare of the sun, and when she looked she saw he was gazing back along the path. His air of expectancy indicated someone was approaching and

Sophie turned to see. Her heart thumped like a drum. A tall blond man, the jacket of his dark grey suit slung over one broad shoulder, was striding energetically towards them. *He* was not boring. *He* was not uninspiring.

'*Guten Tag,*' she said, and heard herself croak.

'Hello,' Diether replied, panting from his exertion. He bent over Rudy to tickle him. 'How's Mr One Tooth?'

The baby's reply was to go off into a paroxysm of delight.

'What are you doing here?' Sophie demanded, grateful to be able to hide behind her dark glasses.

Rudy might be delighted, but she felt edgy. There was only one more evening, one more night to get through, so why, after she had so successfully kept space between them, must Diether appear now?

'I wanted to talk to you so I came home after lunch, but Katrin told me you'd taken Rudy off for a walk.' His chest heaved and he wiped a slick of sweat from his brow. 'For the last half-hour I've been chasing up and down hills, searching for you.'

'What did you want to talk about?' she asked stiffly.

Diether slung his jacket over the back of the bench and sat down beside her. 'You, and me. . .' He paused, catching his breath. 'And Christa.'

Every fibre, every cell of Sophie recoiled. She had no wish to be told that, while his body might traitorously hanker after hers, his heart still belonged to the dead woman. She had not the remotest desire to listen to his confessions, his explanations, nor to any apologies. Indeed, if he asked forgiveness for his emotional permafrost, if he appealed for understanding, he would crucify her.

'No, thank you,' she said curtly, and started to rise.

'You're not going to avoid me again,' Diether said, placing a hand on her arm and restraining her. 'I had intended to talk to you over the weekend, only you disappeared to stay with Eva.'

'It was instead of going on there after I left Bad Godesberg. I've been in Germany far longer than I ever expected, and I want to get home,' Sophie defended.

'Fair enough, but for the past two days you've had Katrin perpetually glued to your side so it was impossible for me to talk to you then.'

'I'm leaving tomorrow,' she said, a sliver of desperation sharpening her voice, 'and I'm not interested in——'

'Not interested in me?' Diether enquired. His indigo eyes seemed to bore straight through her sunglasses. 'You are.'

'Maybe I am—I was,' Sophie adjusted swiftly, her cheeks glowing pink as she realised her mistake, 'but it was never a big deal.'

'So you'd bare your breasts for just any man?'

Her pink cheeks flamed. 'No.'

'And neither would you go to bed with any man,' Diether stated.

'Look, the point is——' Sophie began.

'The point is that when I left your room the other night it wasn't because I'd had second thoughts about how I felt about you or that I'd decided I didn't want to make love to you,' he said, caressing her wrist with the pad of his thumb. 'It was because

I was reluctant to do so knowing that Axel might be lying awake just across the landing. It would've been restrictive and I needed—I need—our first time to be uninhibited and perfect.' Diether gave a lop-sided smile. 'As I thought it was going to be at the hotel.'

She frowned at him. 'If I hadn't stopped everything then, you would have—have continued?' she faltered.

'If Helene's telephone call hadn't stopped everything,' he corrected, 'yes. Sophie, I'm only human and you'd got me so damned inflamed and——'

'What about. . .precautions?' she asked.

'I'd have taken them. Being human doesn't mean I go in for unnecessary risk-taking. About Christa,' he went on.

Sophie wrenched her arm from his grasp. 'Axel told me how you find it difficult to talk about her, and there's no need to do so now. As I just said, I'm leaving in the morning and——'

'There's *every* need,' he interrupted. 'You know why I found it difficult to talk about Christa? It was because I felt so goddamn guilty.'

Her brow creased in confusion. 'Guilty?' she echoed.

'Yes. And note the past tense—I *found* it difficult. What else did Axel say?' he asked.

'Er—only that the two of you had lived together, decided to marry, and then a few months later your wife died.'

'He didn't comment on why we got married?' Diether enquired. 'He didn't tell you Christa was pregnant?'

Sophie looked at him, wide-eyed. 'No.'

'And there would never have been a wedding if she hadn't been.'

Removing her dark glasses, she frowned. By adding these unexpected and startling dimensions to his reminiscences, he had quelled her aversion to listening.

'I think maybe you had better explain,' she said.

Diether stretched out his legs. 'Although it was my suggestion that Christa should move into my apartment—a rash, thoughtless suggestion,' he began slowly, 'I never, ever suggested we should make our relationship legal—because I had doubts about our staying power.'

'And did Christa want to get married?'

'Yes. She never came right out and said so, but she was forever dropping hints. Heavy ones. My doubts turned out to be justified,' he continued, 'because once the novelty had worn off—which took around three months—our affair went flat, stale. The trouble was that, basically, we'd never had much in common, and now long silences developed when we didn't have anything to say to each other.'

'What was Christa like?' Sophie enquired.

'In looks, I suppose she resembled Anna, the girl at the *Karneval* dance. And in personality——' Diether squinted out at the view. 'She'd spend hours with her girlfriends gossiping about fashion and cosmetics—she was a beauty consultant—but she had very little interest in anything more substantial. Topical events were a no-no and so was my career. If I so much as mentioned what I was doing at work or any hopes I had for the future, her eyes'd glaze over. Johannes and she hit it off, and I figure they'd have been far better suited,' he said laconically.

'Anyhow, it'd reached the point where I was gearing myself up to say I wanted us to go our separate ways and please would she move out, when Christa discovered she was pregnant.' He released a slow breath, remembering. 'Which was something I'd never bargained for. Because there clearly was no place for a child in our relationship, I'd been hot on birth control,' he explained. 'She'd opted to go on the Pill, but there were a couple of nights when she neglected to take it.'

'By accident?'

'At the time I wasn't sure, and for a long while I resented the idea that she may have deliberately trapped me. But now I'm more philosophical and I tend to think that, as she insisted, she simply forgot.'

'How did Christa feel about having a baby?' Sophie queried.

'She was pleased—until the sickness started. However, when she told me she was pregnant I said we should get married, which we did, very quickly.'

'You felt it was your duty?'

'To Christa, and to the baby. I also thought I could overcome the fact that our relationship had grown lack-lustre. I was deceiving myself.' Diether frowned down the length of his legs. 'Although previously I'd been working long hours I had eased off when we'd started to live together, but after the wedding I began to spend more time at the office, more time travelling. Christa accused me of being a workaholic, but I wasn't. Although I would've strenuously denied it, I was using business as a means of limiting the time I had to spend with her.' He paused. 'But my absences meant that when she started to suffer from nausea I had no idea of its severity.'

'Axel mentioned Christa's having a rare illness; was the nausea connected with that?' Sophie asked.

'Yes. It was something where the critical problem is becoming dehydrated through sickness, and that's what killed her.' He raised his eyes to hers. 'Afterwards it seemed as though, through my neglect, I'd let Christa and the baby die, and I felt so heartless, so goddamn *guilty*.'

'You believed that if you'd been around more you would've realised she was in danger?'

Diether nodded. 'Also, I kept thinking if I hadn't made her pregnant in the first place, then she would never have become ill. And the knowledge that I'd continued sleeping with her and the baby had been conceived when I was planning to end our affair made it all the worse.'

Sophie's brow puckered. 'Wasn't Christa aware she was becoming dehydrated?'

'No, and neither was the doctor until it was much too late, though it turned out that, for some reason, she was particularly susceptible.'

'So, even if you'd been in constant attendance, there was no reason why you should've been alerted to it either,' she said.

'None.'

'And her becoming pregnant — that was just fate.'

'Yes,' Diether acknowledged, 'and I don't blame myself for anything now. But until a few days ago I did, which is why whenever anyone mentioned my marriage I clammed up.'

'You blamed yourself until just a few days ago?' Sophie protested.

He nodded. 'After Christa died there was a lengthy period when all I did was condemn myself, reproach myself,' he explained, 'but in the end continually harping back wore me out and I pushed what had happened to the back of my mind. As time went on, I decided I'd come to terms with it, though, of course, I hadn't—why else was I so wary of becoming involved with a woman again?'

She cast him a look. 'You mean you haven't had a girlfriend for five years?'

'No, I don't mean that. There was the occasional dalliance and I haven't been entirely celibate,' Diether said drily, 'but I never allowed myself to become emotionally close to anyone. Nor did I ever want to become close. It was only when I met you that——' He stopped and rubbed his fingers over his jaw. 'I'd better tell this in the right order and tell it in full. When you first confronted me and said that Rudy was mine, it seemed as if he was the child I could've had. The child I'd lost.'

Sophie recalled how inwardly distraught he had seemed. 'And it hurt?'

He grimaced. 'It was as though you were stripping away the skin which had been covering a deep and raw wound—which, of course, you were. In a split second, all my unresolved feelings flooded back, and they made me confused and aggressive. One bit of me decided you must be out to trick me, as I half believed Christa had tricked me. Another bit was jealous that my brother had had a son. And the irony of you claiming that an angelic kid like Rudy belonged to Johannes, who'd never achieved anything or done anything worthwhile in his entire life, was not lost on me. A third part——' Diether looked down at the baby who had begun to doze '—very much wished you'd been right and that he was mine. You see, while I'd resented Christa's getting pregnant, I found myself surprisingly enthusiastic about having a son or a daughter. The prospect was pleasurable and endlessly intriguing, and when Christa died I not only mourned her but I mourned the baby too. A friend's wife gave birth in the same week that it had been due, and for over a year I made sure I saw their daughter at regular intervals. And each time I'd think how my child could've been doing the same things, making the same progress.'

'Which is how you knew Rudy wasn't the size of an average nine-month old,' Sophie said.

'That's right. And wishing he was mine was one reason why, when we were at the hospital, I didn't correct the doctor when he assumed I was his father. The possibility that I could be had a definite appeal.' Diether paused. 'The other reason why I failed to correct him was because I liked the idea of him thinking you were my wife.' His blue eyes meshed with hers. 'I liked it very much.'

Sophie's heart fluttered. 'Oh,' she said.

'However, when I realised how drawn I was towards you,' he continued, taking a mental step back, 'I also realised that, one way or another, I needed to sort out my feelings and exorcise Christa's ghost. I made spasmodic attempts, but it wasn't easy and I kept shirking it—until Axel tapped on your door and added his contribution.' He puffed out his cheeks. 'Then thinking things through became imperative. I spent a couple of days dissecting the past and gradually I recognised that, while Christa's death may have been an avoidable tragedy, it was not my fault.'

'And now you feel better?'

He grinned. 'Now I feel great. And now I'm ready to make a proposal.'

'What kind of proposal?' Sophie asked.

'The usual kind.' Diether slid his fingers along her jawline, tilting up her chin with his thumb. 'Will you marry me?'

Her brown-green eyes stretched wide. While he had been giving some exciting and heart-warming clues as to the depth of his feelings, the forthright question came as a surprise.

'M — marry you?' she stammered.

'I know we've only known each other for a short time and I'm not trying to rush you.' He stopped to frown. 'Maybe I am but, hell, I can't let you go back to England without saying *something*. It'll take a few months for us to fix a date and buy a house et cetera, and over those months we'll be getting to know each other better — if you think getting to know each other better is necessary. Personally, I don't,' he said, at speed. 'I don't need any more time to figure out that you're the girl I want to live with for the rest of my life, the girl I want to grow old with, the girl who is good for me, the girl who —— Sophie, *ich liebe dich*,' Diether said, abruptly switching to German in his agitation.

Sophie smiled. 'And I love you, too,' she told him.

'So the answer's yes?'

'*Ja*. Oh, Diether, yes!'

He enfolded her in his arms. 'Thank God,' he said

huskily, 'otherwise I'd have been forced to arrange for Katrin to suffer some debilitating injury.'

'So that I would've needed to stay on?' she asked.

He nodded. 'Why else do you think I turned down those two nannies? I may not have been entirely sure what I was going to do about you, about us, but I knew I couldn't let you disappear.'

Sophie drew back. 'You are a scheming, lying, self-serving rogue,' she informed him.

Diether grinned, wholly unrepentant. 'I was only nurturing our relationship,' he said, and he kissed her.

As his mouth opened on hers, delicious sensation shivered through her. She wound her arms around him, her fingers clutching at the solid muscles of his broad back. They kissed again, and again, and again, their mouths tingling and becoming softly bruised as their passion spiralled.

Eventually Diether pulled away. 'We must stop,' he said, breathing heavily.

'Are you afraid of us disturbing any passing strangers or are you afraid of us disturbing Rudy?' Sophie asked, teasingly.

He cast a glance at the baby who was asleep in the buggy. 'The only person I'm worried about disturbing is me.'

She slid her hand tantalisingly along his thigh. 'Haven't you left it a bit late to worry about that?' she enquired.

Diether closed his eyes and a tremor rippled through him. 'Far too late,' he agreed hoarsely. 'However, much as I would like to make love to you in the open air—and one day I shall,' he said, capturing her questing fingers before she could excite him any further, 'this is not the time and the place.' He sighed. 'And, regrettably, neither is my bed, or your bed tonight.'

'No,' she agreed.

'But when I fly to England with you tomorrow and we go to your house ——'

Sophie smiled. 'We shall be all on our own.'

'So we'll wait until tomorrow, *Liebling*,' he murmured, and kissed her again.

'Until tomorrow,' she said.

Although it had been arranged that her next-door neighbour would come in from time to time to water the plants and pick up the mail, when Sophie opened the front door there was a pile of letters on the mat.

'Ugh, an electricity bill,' she said, bundling them up and starting to sift through, 'and——'

Diether set down the suitcases he was carrying. 'First things first,' he protested.

Their eyes met and clung. The air seemed to pulsate.

'You mean——' Sophie said breathlessly.

'I mean leaving you alone last night was purgatory and if I have to wait a minute longer I shall die.' Patting her bottom, he ushered her towards the stairs. 'Lead the way.'

In the bedroom which had been newly carpeted in dusky pink and decorated with rose-patterned wallpaper, she drew the curtains. Sophie had shed her boots and shrugged off the jacket which covered her jumpsuit when she became aware of Diether's gaze. He had removed his overcoat, but that was all, and now he stood tall and immobile, watching her.

Stricken by a sudden shyness, she gave him a tentative smile.

'Don't take off anything else,' he said, walking towards her. He pressed his lips to the sensitive hollow of her neck. 'I want to undress you.'

Holding the ring of the zip at her neck, Diether began to draw it slowly down, and when she saw the look in his eyes, the intense, leashed male desire, her heart began to pound. The material clung tight and as the zip descended her suit seemed to break open like the pod of a flower, revealing the satiny fullness of her breasts in a white lace bra, the flat plane of her stomach, the tiny white briefs at her hips. He helped her step free from the suit, and then he bent his head to capture her mouth, kissing her fiercely with long, searching kisses. Sophie moulded herself against the length of his body. He felt so strong and so powerful.

'I want to undress you, too,' she murmured, forgetting all about being shy, and he made a sound, feral and acquiescent, in the back of his throat.

Sophie pulled his jacket from his shoulders and dispensed with his tie, then she began to unfasten his shirt. Button after button was released, kiss after kiss was pressed to his chest, until finally she tugged the shirt free. As she ran her hands over his naked torso, Diether trembled.

'Now it's my turn,' he said, his eyes so dark that they were almost black.

Reaching behind her, he unhooked her bra and tossed it aside. Sophie arched towards him, her breasts begging and pleading for his possession.

'Darling,' she sighed, as he began to toy, to

fondle, to roll the straining, sensitive peaks between a thumb and a forefinger. 'Oh, darling!'

This was what she wanted. . .this. . .this.

In time, his hands slid down, drawing the white lace from her hips and brushing across the intimate triangle of dark furze. Sophie closed her eyes, gulped in a breath, then reached for the buckle of his belt.

'Let me help you,' Diether muttered. His trousers and the remainder of his clothes disappeared. 'Hold me,' he begged, as the throbbing heat of his manhood spilled into her hands. He gave a long drawn-out sigh. '*Ye-es.*'

For a moment or two, he stood there, submitting to ever-increasing desire, and then he swung her down with him on to the bed. Sophie felt the quilt cool against her back, his hands moving warmly over her. Diether lowered his head and as he began to stroke his tongue across her nipples she threaded her fingers into the tumbled blond of his hair and held him to her breast. The sensual tug of his mouth, the musky male scent of him, the feel of his naked body against hers was raising her to a level of sexual excitement she had never experienced before. Diether had said he wanted their first time to be uninhibited and perfect, she thought hazily, and it was.

As she made soft murmurs of encouragement, his head lowered and she felt the heated press of his mouth on her stomach, her hips, against the satin-smooth flesh of her inner thigh. She writhed and cried out, a dew flooding between her legs.

'Please,' Sophie begged.

Diether plunged his body into hers and at the

thrust of his maleness she cried out again. Then her thighs were furling around him, drawing him into her, deeper and deeper. Lost in desire, she bit at the hard smoothness of his shoulder, whimpering and making small, wild noises. She drew her hands down his spine and, reaching the tautness of his buttocks, she pressed him into her.

'Please,' Sophie murmured again, her fingernails flexing into his flesh. 'Please.'

With a groan, he began to move, his hips grinding against hers in a driving, pulsating rhythm. Her eyes closed, she clung, quivering with intensity and almost weeping at the power of the emotions which had claimed her. Now all she knew was his supple, muscular body on her yielding, open one, a tangle of hair, perspiration sleeked over heated skin, a deep inner welling of moisture. Diether groaned again — a low, guttural sound of ecstasy — and then he made her his.

Tenderly Diether stroked his hand over her breast, her stomach, the triangle of dark hair between her legs, not to arouse her — they were too sated for that — but as a gesture of love and protection.

'You were going to take a look at your letters,' he reminded her.

Lazily, Sophie reached out to gather up the bundle of mail which had been dropped on the bedside table more than an hour ago. She discarded the electricity bill, plus a couple of what were obviously circulars, and had a look at her bank statement. Good, she remained solvent. As she came to the next envelope, she frowned. The bulky airmail envelope was postmarked Mississippi and she recognised the childish writing.

'It's from Lisette,' she said, and frowned at him across the pillow. 'I know I said she wouldn't change her mind about Rudy, but suppose —'

'Don't get alarmed,' Diether said soothingly. 'Just open it.'

Sitting up, Sophie ripped open the envelope and tipped out the papers which were inside. There was a typed document and a three-page letter which her erstwhile lodger had written. She read the letter first.

'Lisette's become a member of a religious commune and has moved in with them. On a permanent basis, she reckons. She says it's a wonderful place, the people are friendly and already she feels at home. She has a job working in their handicraft shop where they sell —' As her eyes flicked over to the next page, she continued to pick out sentences which gave the general gist, but abruptly her recital slowed. 'She's told the commune's leader about how she left Rudy with me, and he's insisted that as her intention is to relinquish all claim to him she must do so officially and legally. So this —' she tapped the typed document '— is a signed statement to that effect which has been prepared by a lawyer.'

Diether pushed himself up against the pillow. 'Why don't we adopt Rudy?' he suggested. 'If Lisette's relinquishing all claim she shouldn't raise any objection, though now that you have her address we can write and ask her.'

Sophie gazed at him. 'You'd be happy to do that? You'd be willing for him to live with us?'

'Sure. It would give him security and a stronger

sense of belonging. Plus you're devoted to him, he's a great little kid and I am his uncle.'

'A wonderful uncle,' she declared, throwing her arms around him and kissing him. 'And a wonderful lover.'

'Flattery will get you everywhere, especially if you press your naked breasts against me,' Diether murmured, for in the fervour of her embrace the sheet which had been covering her had slithered down between them.

Sophie grinned, drawing away. 'I'd better read the signed statement.'

He heaved a noisy sigh. 'If you must.'

'It all seems straightforward enough to me, but what do you think?' she asked, passing it to him.

'I can't read it without my glasses,' Diether protested, and he climbed out of bed to pick up his jacket and find his spectacle case. 'Everything appears to be comprehensively covered,' he agreed, when he had looked through. 'Do you know a good solicitor?'

She nodded. 'The man who handled my grandfather's affairs.'

'Suppose we go and see him tomorrow, and set the adoption ball rolling?' Diether suggested. 'And then when our children arrive they'll have a big brother ready and waiting.'

'Our children?' Sophie queried, savouring the phrase.

'I reckon we should have a few, don't you? Though not for a couple of years.'

'Yes, I do, but ——' she tilted a brow ' — how many is a few?'

'Three? Four?' Diether traced a question mark between her breasts. 'Six?'

She laughed. 'Suppose we leave it open to negotiation?' she said, and kissed him again.

'You're steaming up my glasses,' he murmured, as the kiss began to lengthen.

With a sigh, Sophie pulled back to lift the spectacles from his nose and put them aside. 'I should've known there'd be drawbacks to marrying an old man,' she said.

'I'm not old,' Diether protested. 'I'm in my prime.'

'Who says?'

'Me, and haven't I just proved it?' he demanded.

She rubbed the end of her nose against his. 'Overwhelmingly. What do we do about Katrin?' she asked, all of a sudden.

'What do *you* want to do?' he responded. 'Do you want to start a fresh career?'

'No, I'd rather look after Rudy — and you.'

'So we'll tell her that we're sorry, but once we're married we shan't be requiring her services.' Diether grinned. 'To be honest, I wouldn't have wanted a third person around. After all, Rudy will be in bed so he's not going to be bothered if we decide to strip off and make love in front of the fire one evening, but a nanny could be.'

'*Would* be,' Sophie said, with a grin. 'I think our bringing up Rudy will be a weight off Helene's mind,' she added, growing serious.

'Very much so, and it's not as though he'll be far away. She can see him whenever she wishes, and he can go and stay with her from time to time. For example, he can stay when I go abroad on business and you accompany me. I'm sure when I go to Italy Signor Angellino will be delighted to see you — as he was when you made your appearance in my office that day,' Diether added drolly.

She thought back to their first meeting. 'I know I lied and claimed we were friends, but desperate people do desperate things and getting in to see you seemed to be as difficult as. . .breaking down the Berlin Wall.'

'That hard?'

'Harder,' she vowed.

'I happened to be visiting Berlin when the bulldozers moved in on the Wall and it was a memorable occasion, though not as memorable as the one which took place quarter of an hour ago,' he said huskily.

Sophie smiled. 'But now the Wall's crumbled and the two Germanys are united, and we're united, too.'

'Forever and ever. Mind you, there's always room for a spot of active reunification.'

'You have something in mind?' she asked.

'I do,' Diether said, and drew her down with him back between the sheets.

CHAPTER TEN

THE factory manager was in his element. He had a weakness for pretty women and an abiding interest in his work, and now he could combine the two for he was telling his employer's new wife about the engineering processes which he controlled. Frau von Lössingen was a charmer, he thought, and the baby his boss carried—apparently that loafer Johannes's kid—was a beguiling little thing, too.

As the manager talked, Sophie listened intently. Much of what he said was technical, but he sounded so proud, so pleased and so dedicated, that she felt she must make the effort to follow—and to ask sensible questions.

'Apart from your wanting to see what goes on, that was a splendid exercise in public relations,' Diether remarked, when he had finished showing her around the complex and they were walking out to the car.

Sophie looked at him. 'What do you mean?'

'I reckon you've bewitched just about every male in the place and Rudy's bewitched every female.'

She laughed. 'Anything to keep your workforce happy.'

'Never mind the workforce, it's me you should be thinking about,' he protested, curving an arm around her and pulling her to a halt. 'A kiss might just do it.'

She reached up and kissed him on the mouth. 'Happy now?' she asked.

Diether grinned. 'In orbit.'

'You're easily pleased,' Sophie said, her eyes shining.

'By you,' he agreed, his gaze soft upon her, and, hand in hand, they started walking again.

As they reached the Mercedes, she turned to face the office building. 'Von Lössingen,' she said, showing Rudy the golden letters which adorned the wall. 'That's your name.'

'Officially,' Diether told him, 'because you're now officially our son and we're officially your mummy and daddy,' he said, and shared a smile with Sophie. 'What do you think of that?'

The baby took hold of his tie in a chubby fist. 'Blah,' he said, and chuckled.

GERMANY

THE RHINE VALLEY

The countryside along the banks of the Rhine is among the most picturesque to be seen in the whole of Europe: visitors come from far and wide to admire the romantic scenery—mountains, vineyards and fairy-tale castles—which has inspired myriad legends and moved writers such as Lord Byron and Victor Hugo to record its visual poetry. Such a setting will surely inspire any modern-day lovers as they uncover the delights of this magical valley and its proud city of Bonn.

THE ROMANTIC PAST. . .

The **River Rhine** is 820 miles long, flowing from twin sources in the Swiss mountains to its mouth in the North Sea. It is a river steeped in romance; for example, on its journey from **Bingen** to **Koblenz** the river narrows, twisting and turning to form the 'Rhine gorge'; the potentially dangerous currents in these waters gave rise to the legend of the blonde enchantress on the Loreley cliff, who bewitched boatmen with her song, luring them to certain death.

Bonn served as West Germany's seat of Federal Government from 1949, when the country was set up, to 1991. This status as 'provisional capital' resulted in the doubling of its size through its absorption of several surrounding villages and its intake of diplomats, although its population is still under 300,000 and its historical character is unspoilt.

Bonn's most famous son is **Ludwig van Beethoven**, the composer, whose birthplace at Bonngasse 20 has been turned into an impressive museum of his life and work, displaying portraits, manuscripts, letters and instruments.

South of Bonn lie the **Siebengebirge**, or seven mountains, around which much Rhinish folklore is based: 'Snow-White and the Seven Dwarfs' is said to be set here, and the most famous hills of the range, the **Drachenfels**, we are told, saw the slaying of a dragon by Siegfried, hero of Nibelung legend. He subsequently bathed in its blood, and a wine called Drachenblut (dragon's blood) is still made in the vineyards below the majestic remains of the 12th century castle there.

The epitome of Rhine romanticism is the **Rolandsbogen** ruin, below which stands a convent. Legend has it that Roland, the most famous knight of the Emperor Charlemagne, built the castle in order that he could gaze down on his beloved Hildegard, who had taken the veil when mistakenly told of his death.

THE ROMANTIC PRESENT — pastimes for lovers. . .

Bonn is one of Europe's greenest cities, where there
are lots of opportunities for walking hand in hand
through its 1,200 parks and gardens — relax in the
peaceful surroundings of the **Botanical Gardens** or
stroll down the kilometre-long avenue of chestnut
trees leading to the Popplesdorf, now part of the
university.

The Romantic period of music is not only repre-
sented by Beethoven's first home, but also by the
Beethovenhalle, a futuristic building overlooking the
Rhine and staging outstanding classical concerts. In
addition, the music-lover will enjoy the **Robert
Schumann House**, containing memorabilia of this
composer, much of whose passionate songs were
inspired by his love for his wife, the pianist Clara
Wieck. Sadly, he suffered a mental breakdown, and
tried to kill himself by throwing himself into the
Rhine two years before his actual death in a
sanatorium.

The skull of the **Neanderthal Man**, c.60,000 years
old and found near Düsseldorf, can be seen in the
city's best museum, the **Landesmuseum**, whose other
treasures include a stunning collection of Roman
and Frankish jewellery and a mosaic dedicated to
the sun.

Bonn's focal point is the market place, or **markt**,
where you'll be enchanted by the Baroque **rathaus**
(town hall), built in 1737 and dominating the town
centre with its pink façade. During the **Bonn**

Summer Festival this building hosts numerous cultural events, and for the rest of the time you can browse in the square's daily market.

If you're lucky enough to be in the area some time between November and Lent, you and your loved one can join the fun of the **carnival**, a lavish celebration held every year and at its craziest in the city of Cologne, just north of Bonn. Costume balls, dinners, processions and galas present the onlooker with a riotous spectacle of colour and music, and not to be missed is the climax of the celebrations — the Rose Monday Parade, involving 7,000 people and three hundred horses, during which forty tons of sweets, flowers and eau de Cologne containers are thrown to the crowd! The whole is wonderful fun and a great chance to dress up and let your hair down!

Cologne is well worth a visit during *Karneval* or not, being one of West Germany's oldest and most dignified cities as well as one of its most beautiful. For the best view of the city and the Rhine, climb up to the steeple of the **Dom**, the vast Gothic cathedral and its greatest landmark. Walk southwest of it and you will come to the pedestrianised area along the Hohe Strasse, which, with its charming outdoor cafés, has a curiously French feel, or head for a taste of old-town Cologne between the Gross St Martin church and the Deutzer bridge: here there is a thriving neighbourhood centred on masterfully restored houses built in the 13th and 14th centuries, and you will want to spend hours exploring its delightful art galleries, restaurants and antique shops.

German cooking is generally excellent value and of a high quality, especially if you find an establishment serving *Gutbürgerliche Kuche*, hearty home-made food. National favourites include **Pumpernickel** (black rye bread) with cold meats and cheeses at breakfast, and **Sauerkraut** (pickled green cabbage), served with any variation of pork, on which German main courses are invariably based, such as **Bratwurst** or **Schnitzel**. To finish you can indulge in pastries or **Apfelstrudel**. Delicious!

The Rhine Valley is world-famous for its wines, and the best known region is the **Rheingau** opposite Bingen, south of Bonn, where you can see the vineyards that produce the Riesling grape, one of the greatest white varieties. The wine villages scattered along the banks of the river and its tributaries can be enjoyably explored on foot, and will give you the opportunity to work up a good thirst in order to do justice to the local vintages!

To soak up the unique atmosphere of the Rhine in the most romantic way, we suggest that you and your partner take a boat trip; from your vantage point at the very heart of the valley you will be able to step back into the chivalrous past during which were built the magnificent castles before your eyes — **Burg Klopp**, **Ehrenfels**, **Reichenstein** and **Heimburg Castles**, to name but a few. Its thirty-one castles and ruins surely guarantee the Rhine valley as being the most romantic in the world!

DID YOU KNOW THAT . . .?

*   **eau de Cologne**, now internationally known as a toilet water, was originally, in the 18th century, meant to be an aphrodisiac

*   Bonn has the highest percentage of **dogs** per head of population in the whole of West Germany

*   the currency unit is the **Deutschmark**

*   when a German says '*Ich liebe dich*' he's telling you he loves you!

POSTCARDS FROM EUROPE

HARLEQUIN PRESENTS®

Travel across Europe in 1994 with Harlequin Presents. Collect a new *Postcards From Europe* title each month!

Don't miss
DARK SUNLIGHT
by Patricia Wilson
Harlequin Presents #1644

Available in April, wherever Harlequin Presents books are sold.

HPPFE4

Hi—

The sun was shining brightly here in Spain until I met Felipe de Santis. The man is used to giving orders and doesn't respect my abilities as a journalist. But I'm going to get my story—and I'm going to help Felipe's sister!

Love, Maggie

P.S. If only I could win Felipe's love....

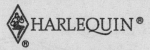

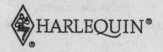

Harlequin proudly presents four stories about *convenient* but not *conventional* reasons for marriage:

- ♦ To save your godchildren from a "wicked stepmother"

- ♦ To help out your eccentric aunt—and her sexy business partner

- ♦ To bring an old man happiness by making him a grandfather

- ♦ To escape from a ghostly existence and become a real woman

Marriage By Design—four brand-new stories by four of Harlequin's most popular authors:

CATHY GILLEN THACKER
JASMINE CRESSWELL
GLENDA SANDERS
MARGARET CHITTENDEN

Don't miss this exciting collection of stories about marriages of convenience. Available in April, wherever Harlequin books are sold.